'[Sedgwick's] complex, beautifully written novel draws
haunting contrasts between Russia's myth and its harsh
reality.' *Financial Times*

. . . imes

. . . omising, a thoroughly

BLOOD RED
SNOW WHITE

Кровь красная, Снег белый

Marcus Sedgwick

Orion Children's Books

First published in Great Britain in 2007
by Orion Children's Books
Paperback edition first published in Great Britain in 2008
by Orion Children's Books
a division of the Orion Publishing Group Ltd
Orion House
5 Upper Saint Martin's Lane
London WC2H 9EA
An Hachette Livre UK Company

1 3 5 7 9 10 8 6 4 2

The extract from *Old Peter's Russian Tales* is reproduced here with
kind permission of Jane Nissen Books.
All telegrams have been sourced from and reproduced here
with kind permission of the National Archive.

The right of Marcus Sedgwick to be identified as the author of this work
has been asserted.

A catalogue record for this book is available from the British Library

Printed in Great Britain by Clays Ltd, St Ives plc

ISBN 978 1 84255 637 5

For Alice

'Russian fairyland is quite different. Under my windows the wavelets of the Volkhov are beating quietly in the dusk. A gold light burns on a timber raft floating down the river. Beyond the river in the blue midsummer twilight are the broad Russian plain and the distant forest. Somewhere in that great forest of trees – a forest so big that the forests of England are little woods beside it – is the hut where old Peter sits at night and tells these stories to his grandchildren.'

From *Old Peter's Russian Tales* by Arthur Ransome

Contents

1942 — Coniston

The years slip away.

Outside, down at the lake, I can hear the water lapping and the geese calling. From the woods above the house comes the soft roar of a shotgun – someone hunting in the dusk.

In here, the fire flickers brightly, and my chair is old and comfortable. Surely this is home.

And yet, the years slip away.

Opposite me, the chair by the fire is empty.

Everyone should have someone to share their fireside, especially an old fool like me.

Time unwinds, and I am a young man in Russia once more: as if I were lifting the lid on a box of keepsakes, the memories return; many of happiness, some of sorrow. As if I threw wide a door that leads to a room long abandoned, but once familiar, I am back in another world, a world in which I was another man. And those who think I am an old fool, and those who thought I was a silly young fool, may never know who I really was, and how I fought.

1

Let me tell you a fairy tale.

I used to tell stories like this all the time; it used to be so important. It even saved my life once. Now let me see, how do fairy tales begin?

Part One

A Russian Fairy Tale

Русская сказка

Once upon a time ...

Beyond the sunrise, half way to the moon, and so very far away it would make your feet weep to think about it, lies a land vast in size and deep in sadness. From where we sit, on the far edge of history, we can see across Time itself, and yet this land is so big we struggle to see all of it at once.

Nevertheless, here it is: here's a river as wide as a sea, and into it flows a stream as wide as a river. In summer salmon leap through the cool fresh water, in winter the ice is as thick as a house is tall.

There's a forest as large as a country, and in the heart of the forest is a single hut, from where we see a man, an old man with a great grey beard, staggering out in the winterdeep snow. He carries an axe slung on his back, for he's a woodcutter, and despite the snow, he has to keep his orphaned grandchildren warm. He doesn't see the bear padding through the snow just half a league away, but neither does the bear see him, and in the remote depths of the forest, half a league is as good as a thousand.

There! Away at the sunset edge of the land; soldiers! Soldiers in their millions, fighting a great war which seems to be without end. We know that it will end, one day, when enough of them are dead, but the soldiers do not. They have fought for so long they have forgotten what it is they are dying for. Look! Another one is killed; the top of his head blown clean off by a bullet at close range. His hot red blood freezes before it even reaches the ground.

And there's a man, a young man, a stranger to the land, who is foolish enough to think he can walk across its endlessness.

Remember him. He carries a small leather suitcase in one hand and a strange but sturdy wooden box in the other. In his heart there is pain, but in his head there is wonder; wonder and a delightful tumble of words he has been trying to learn. Russian words.

For this is Russia.

A Magical Land

The woodcutter, having missed the bear, came home to his grandchildren, his little boy and girl, and, because nothing made them happier in the world, he told them a fairy tale.

As always, the moment he came through the door stamping the snow off his boots they jumped up and began to pester him for a story.

'All in good time, Little Pigeons,' he laughed, 'just as soon as we've had our soup!'

So they ate their steaming soup and thick black bread, and when they were done, Old Peter the woodcutter told his grandchildren a fairy tale. The tale he told them is the one I am telling you now, and it's the story of the Tsar, the man who ruled over the whole great country.

Just the word, Tsar, tells you how powerful he was, because of where it comes from. Some people spell it Tsar, others Czar, and if spelled that way you begin to see another word, the word from which it grew; Caesar. Those Roman Emperors ruled many lands, but our Tsar holds sway over one hundred and eighty million people. Imagine. One hundred and eighty million people, maybe three times the number that Augustus or Marcus Aurelius ruled.

An Empire this large needs a powerful Tsar. That is what the Tsar's father told him when he was just a little boy, a little boy called Nicky. And when Nicky's father, Alexander, was little, that's exactly what his father had told him too. This is the truth and they know it, because God has told them so.

How else could you rule a land so very, very big? Only a sharp and decisive man, with a single vision, can keep hold of something as massive as Russia, and as magical. For it is not simply its size that makes it so cumbersome, but its superstition. Even the Imperial symbol is a mythical beast – a fabulous double-headed eagle, that looks both ways at once.

Up in the city, on the banks of the mighty river Neva, sits the Chamber of Wonders created by Peter the Great; a museum he founded in an attempt to dispel the superstitions of the peasants.

There, hidden in drawers and on display in glass-fronted cabinets, are hideous things. Monsters, freaks and ghouls. Stuffed and mounted, a sheep with two heads, and snakes with two tails. Monkeys with three arms, a stillborn lamb with eight legs. These are the stuff of nightmares and they are also the seed of fairy tale monsters, but they are nothing to what is in that final cabinet, the one in the corner of the room. You saw it from the edge of your eye as you came in, saw the crowds flocking around it, heard their awed silence. Even now you find your feet pulling you over to it unwillingly, your eyes refusing to shut though your heart is praying they will close for ever.

There in the case; dead things. Things that might have lived once, maybe for a year, maybe just for an hour, maybe born dead. Their skin bleached by preservative salts, their faces contorted as if shrieking in horror at themselves, screaming for all eternity as if they caught sight of their reflection in a looking glass. Their faces scream as the crowd should, but does not. Babies with two heads, like the sheep. Unborn Siamese twins, with two legs but two heads and four arms. A foetus with no head at all, but countless arms, like an octopus.

Peter, the Great, the moderniser, decreed that all these monstrosities should be brought to his city, to show they were natural, not magical. He wanted to show that in the vastness of his empire there was nothing but nature's law. He wanted science to spread light like the sun over the winter forest. But his efforts achieved exactly the opposite, and people gasped and crossed themselves and pressed their noses against the glass until it became opaque with grease.

He tried to take the magic from Russia, but the magic would not go. Even the names of places tell you that magic is as much a part of this land as the soil or the river water: Irkutsk. The Caspian Sea. The Sea of

Okhotsk, the Sea of Japan. Kazan, Murmansk, Kharkov and Vladivostok.

There is magic in those words, just as there was tragedy in the blood of the Tsar and his family.

A tragedy that was a hundred years in the making.

Life and Blood

There was tragedy all across Europe.

Tragedy in the shape of war.

If you looked at the family trees of the royal houses of Europe, you would find more threads between them than in a busy spider's web. The Tsar had a cousin who was a king of another country. His name was George. Nicholas, the Tsar, and George had another cousin, William, the Kaiser, who had gone to war against Nicholas and George's countries. It made no sense, but then when has a war made sense?

Let me return to the fairy tale, of the Tsar and his people. The Tsar was in trouble, for his was a story nearing its end.

For three centuries the Tsar's family had ruled like gods over their empire. From time to time there had been an outbreak of opposition, as some foolish soul tried to upset the old order, but each and every time, that order had been restored.

11

So the Tsar lived with his family still. He had a wife, Alexandra, who he called Alix, just as she called him Nicky from the time when they had fallen in love. They lived in a beautiful palace, in fact, they lived in many beautiful palaces. Each was more sumptuous than the other, but there was one special palace, prized the highest; Tsarskoe Selo. Here they lived with their beautiful children, four daughters; Olga, Tatiana, Maria, Anastasia, and their only son, the boy of great sorrow, Alexei.

Alexei, who carries his sorrow, and Russia's tragedy, in his blood.

They wanted for nothing. In the same way that the Tsars and all their families had wanted for nothing down the centuries, every wish that could be dreamt of the Tsar granted his blessed wife and children.

Our woodcutter and his grandchildren could never have begun to even imagine the splendour of the imperial palaces. Where the woodcutter had three spoons, of wood, one for himself, one for his grandson Vanya and one for his granddaughter Maroosia, the palace had a thousand spoons of silver. Where the woodcutter had three chairs, the palace had four hundred, of gold. And where he had the clothes he stood in and the boots he wore, the Tsarina had ten thousand dresses of satin and silk. Of billowing satin and silk too were the coverings for the beds in the royal chambers, where the woodcutter and his grandchildren had a single old woollen blanket each. The Tsarina had jewels too! Ropes of pearls, long strings, with the most perfect moon-white pearls to hang about her pretty neck. And diamonds! Diamonds by the bucketful, which she kept in a peculiar, small, green leather case.

Even when they sat down to take tea, they did it in style. The Tsarina had a favourite little samovar in which they boiled water for their tea, or rather, their servants did. But the Tsarina loved to pour the hot water into the cups herself, because the samovar was special. It was solid silver, and shone like the white sun low over a frozen lake on a winter's morning, and on its side were her initials in English, the language she and Nicky would write to each other in; AR, Alexandra Romanov.

The woodcutter knew none of this, but went through the woods each day, still unaware of the lurking bear.

And the children? What of them? The Tsar's children had everything they could ask for. Each had a whole room of toys to play with, and they shared not one but a whole stable of rocking horses. Far away in the forest Vanya and Maroosia had nothing, but still they were happy, as they had each other, and their little black cat and tall grey wolf-dog to play with. And they had Grandfather to feed them and keep them warm and tell them fairy tales at bedtime.

I said that the Tsar's children had rocking horses, but that is not quite true; the girls had horses, Olga and Tatiana, Maria and Anastasia, but their young brother, Alexei, did not. Nor did he have a bicycle of his own, nor a bat and ball. He was not allowed to run and play as his sisters did, and he was not allowed to play with the palace dogs.

And why? Not because his mother and father loved him any less than his sisters, but for a different reason. The tragedy in his blood. For there, in his veins, passed down from his grandmother, now long dead but once the Queen of the British Empire, skulked an evil disease.

The disease was a strange thing, that no one could explain. Maybe even strange enough to put Alexei into Peter's Chamber of Wonders, if he were to die. For when the young Tsarevich cut himself, the bleeding would not stop.

Maybe it doesn't sound so serious. You or I might cut ourselves, nicking our hand on the tooth of the saw as we cut logs for the fire. We might take God's name, but think no more of it. You or I might catch the back of our hand against the bread knife as we pass a hunk of black bread across the table in the hut. We might sing to ignore it, but think no more of it. In a few moments the cut would stop bleeding, and we would go on with our soup and stories.

But the Tsarevich, little Alexei, was different. If he cut himself, no matter in how small a way, there would be pandemonium in the palace. His mother would shriek and call for the nurses, the nurses would come and call for the doctors and all would fly around in useless panic, as the cut refused to heal and slowly, but surely, the boy's blood would pour from his body.

One day, Alexei scratched his ear on a thorn. It took three days for the blood to stop. So, as he grew, he was forbidden from doing anything that might endanger him. No rocking horses, no rough games, no running. No fun.

There could be no risk to his life. He was not the first in his family to suffer from the disease. There was an uncle who'd had it too. Alexei had never known him, because at the age of three he'd fallen through a window. His body bled on the inside and he never recovered. The Tsar and the Tsarina determined that this must never happen to their son, their only son, and therefore the only future Tsar of Russia. He had to live, so that one day he would rule the Empire, as his family had done for three hundred years.

He *had* to live.

In the Name of the Tsar

The Tsar worried. He worried like no other Tsar before him. He looked inwards and he worried about his family, about Alexei and his strange blood. He looked outward and he worried about his empire.

What he saw disturbed him.

There was deep poverty, and famine. People were going hungry and were growing angry. Small disturbances on the farms where the peasants worked got out of hand, there had been riots and soldiers had been sent to restore order.

It had happened during his grandfather's time, and his father's. Trying to make the workers' lives better, they had decided to introduce reforms, to give them certain freedoms so that they might earn just a bit more money, to allow them to sell some of what they grew rather then giving it all to the landowner.

The Tsar looked at his people and what he saw disturbed him. He saw clearly what was wrong.

His father and his grandfather had been weak.

They had been indulgent, and now the people were

trying to take more than they were entitled to.

'I will never agree to what they want,' he declared, 'because I consider it harmful to the people whom God has entrusted to me.'

He knew what he had to do.

He repealed the reforms and sent soldiers to quell any trouble as soon as it started.

The people's hunger grew worse, and as winter began to bite at their heels, they grew cold too. Death rode through Russia on a pale horse, taking everyone he could with sickness and famine, and the people grew afraid, and with their fear came more anger. Though the Tsar believed he had restored order, he had not stopped the dark mutterings in hidden corners of his empire.

Seeing the trouble that was boiling up, one young priest decided he had to act.

'Father', the people called him, though he was father to no one.

'Father,' they said, 'what shall we do? Our children are starving, and dying. We are starving and sick. But what can we do? We are nothing. The Tsar owns us as he would a horse, but cares less for us than those beasts. Help us, Father!'

The young priest heard them and replied.

'We will act, together. Let us go into the city hand in hand, to the very gates of the palace. This Sunday, one hundred thousand of us must march and there we will make our case to the Tsar.'

The people looked at him, uncertainly, for though

17

they wanted to believe they could do such a thing, they couldn't believe it was possible. The priest, whose name was Georgy, saw the doubt on their faces.

'Believe me,' he said. 'Go to your families now, and to the houses of your friends, and tell them that there must be one hundred thousand of us when Sunday comes. Tell them this, and there will be.'

So they went and told their friends and their families, and everybody told someone else that Sunday would be the day when their lives would change, and in the meantime, Georgy thought about what he had started. What would happen on Sunday? Suppose no one came? Suppose *everyone* came? It was his doing. He had given the people hope and it was his responsibility. Suppose the Tsar didn't take any notice of them?

But he had to. He had to! And just in case he didn't, Georgy decided to write a letter to the Tsar, to give him on the day. It would be as if one hundred thousand people had handed the letter to the Tsar personally. No one could ignore a letter like that.

On Saturday night he sat down to write it. It was a long letter, polite and respectful, and it was passionate and proud. He asked the Tsar to care for his people, to see their troubles and to take them away, to bring good things to Russia.

When he had finished writing, Georgy sat back in his chair. He had written for an hour and it was late. He rose and took his candle to bed, blew it out and lay in the dark, dreaming of the day to come, and dreamed that no one came. In his sleep, he alone stood quaking before the Tsar, and when he handed over the letter, he saw with horror that he was holding a blank sheet of paper.

The priest need not have worried.

When Sunday came, it was possibly more than one hundred thousand people who flocked into the streets of the city. They joined in a massive throng, and began to walk towards the Winter Palace. As they went, they sang, and the crowd was so very large that many different songs were all sung at once. Here and there the words and melodies mixed with each other, but no one cared. There were women and children in the crowd too, and there was laughter and hope and comradeship. A tired mother gratefully let her daughter ride on the shoulders of a tough old veteran, the washer-women from the Neva walked like princesses alongside the sailors, until at last the one hundred thousand surged into the Palace Square, so that Georgy could hand his letter to the Tsar.

In the square, the Tsar had his answer already waiting. Even before Georgy had a chance to hand over his letter, the Tsar gave his reply.

A thousand soldiers stood outside the palace gates.

A thousand soldiers knelt in the snow, and lifted their rifles to their shoulders.

A thousand shots scorched the air, and the blood began to flow.

They screamed and they ran.

The young priest ran too. As he ran, the letter fell from his hand, where it was trampled underfoot by one hundred thousand pairs of feet.

Cruel tales

S ome fairy tales are cruel, like the last one. Sometimes
there is no happy ending, where the brave young
peasant marries the beautiful princess, and wins a trunk-
ful of treasure to boot. What happens in a fairy tale is
no more or less in anyone's control than what happens
in life. What should have happened in the last story?
How should it have ended?

Maybe it was not the end of the story at all. Perhaps
the Tsar thought it was, but didn't realise that what he
had done would lead to a very different ending indeed.

Even in a tale with a happy ending, there may be
sadness on the way. Think of Vanya and Maroosia. They
are happy children, they love their grandfather, and
they love their little cat and big dog. But they have no
parents. Their parents died years before our story starts.
What awful thing takes both parents away from their
children? Maybe you don't want to know, and maybe it
doesn't matter. But it was the Tsar who killed them.

Not with his own hands, but just as surely, the Tsar killed their parents. He made serfs of them, made them move to work on his lands, and then worked them so hard that Father died of exhaustion and Mother died of a broken heart.

Engagement and Escape

Wait!
There!

It's the bear again, prowling through the flawless snows, heavy and heavy and heavy, paws and claws and teeth and fur. Thick, thick fur.

He is moving again, but as yet without purpose. Dimly he hears the commotion from the city, the gunfire and the stampeding feet, but it means nothing to him yet. He wanders through the trees as if asleep, or in a waking dream, unclear of what he is and what he will be. He is mighty, almost unbelievably powerful in fact, but like a gentle giant, he doesn't know his own strength.

Not yet.

Not yet, but soon.

The bear stumbles back to a hidden cave who knows where in the forest, to hibernate. He goes to sleep, an enchanted sleep, as in a fireside tale.

He sleeps for twelve years.

And for now, our story lies elsewhere.

Do you remember the stranger? The young stranger, with the suitcase in one hand and the wooden box in the other. Wearing an old soldier's greatcoat to armour himself against the cold, he's still walking through Russia, but he has left the forest behind him now and is approaching the city. There are many fairy tales already about him, and by the time he is an old man there will be many more, but let me tell you the story about the stranger, and Ivy.

The young man had been born, across the water, in the big open country called the Lakes, because that's just what you find nestled between the hills and fells where he lived. He'd lived in this beautiful tough land all his childhood, and had gone to school with ugly rough boys on the shores of his favourite lake.

One winter, when he was barely more than a toddler, his father was visited by a Russian prince, a man with the splendid name of Kropotkin. After they had concluded their business, the prince was appalled to find that the child could not ice-skate, and there and then took him out to a frozen river and guided his infant steps. It's a fairy tale in itself. A tale with a happy ending, how, when he got to the big school by the lake, he suffered at the hands of the other boys, bigger and stronger than him. And meaner. Every day, as they fought and played their way through their school days,

24

he'd be punished for being weak. Until the day, when, in the midst of the hardest winter in thirty years, the lake on whose shores the school stood froze over. None of the other boys had seen such ice before, and the head-master declared that school was shut and all games should be played on the ice.

The lake froze solid for four weeks on end. Perch were trapped like flies in aspic; they looked dead, but maybe they miraculously came back to life when the steely ice finally thawed. At last the headmaster's obsession with sport worked in the boy's favour. Every day the boys would stay out on the ice until dusk, when bonfires were lit on the shores to warm them through. Here, finally, was one thing he could do bet-ter than the others. For the rest of his life he remembered the relief of gliding past his tormentors floundering on their backsides while he headed off, the whole glittering world beneath his skates, thanks to Kropotkin.

That's a tale with a happy ending, and one that shows there is no such thing in life as chance, or luck. There is only fate. Which is why, years later, when the young man walked into Russia, he could have gone nowhere else. It was his fate to go there.

But I was telling you another story, about Ivy, and how the young man ended up in Russia at all.

He grew up. He left school and the Lakes, and, now

a man, he moved to the big city in the South. And there he fell in love.

Not once, but hundreds of times. He developed a habit of falling in love at least once a week, and of asking whoever the girl was to marry him.

This went well for a year or so, because all the girls he asked to marry him said no. There were narrow scrapes from time to time; once he thought better of the marriage proposal he'd written in a letter, and travelled a hundred miles to intercept it before the girl could read it. The girls had a fair idea of his nature, that he was young and impetuous, and so they said no, though they did it kindly, and with a quick peck on his cheek.

But then, one day, one of them said yes.

Her name was Ivy, and the young man had fallen in love with her straight away. It would have been rude not to, because all the other young men in the city also wanted her. She was beautiful and witty, and she was much more fun than other girls. He wrote poems for her and about her, and they got married.

They enjoyed the whole thing so much they got married again two weeks later, on All Fool's Day.

After their honeymoon was over, they moved out of the city and into a cottage in the countryside, and there they did what comes easily to newlyweds, and the result was a baby. A baby girl. They called her Tabitha.

Then life changed. There never was a story that was happy through and through, and this one is no different. The young man began to realise that he had not married the woman he thought he had.

She began to change, or maybe it's closer to say that she became herself.

As if he had married an enchantress, a crone who had transformed into a beauty, her true colours began to emerge.

The young man saw that Ivy was like a fairy tale herself. She lived in a world of fantasy. Maybe she had become bored, maybe she missed her life in the city, maybe he and Tabitha weren't enough for her. So she made up stories of her own. She told him that other men wanted her still. She admitted to having affairs, though all these stories were just fantasies.

The young man worried about her but decided that it was probably best to ignore the tales. Ivy's stories got worse. She told him that she had discovered a plot against her honour. Three coarse men, she had learned, were planning to kidnap her and hold her against her will (sort of) in a lighthouse. She told him to buy a gun to defend her.

He thought for a while, trying to remember a lighthouse within a hundred miles of where they lived. He didn't buy a gun.

And the young man, meanwhile, had fallen in love again. This time, however, he'd fallen in love with someone quite unexpected; he had fallen in love with his daughter. This was something he had not been prepared for, as he was swept up by a bond and a yearning and a protectiveness for which he found words were quite inadequate.

Now, after all the marriage proposals he had made, and years with Ivy, he at last understood what love truly is. Love, he decided, is not about how much someone else cares for you, it's about how much you care for someone else, and he cared for Tabitha very much indeed. He smiled, as if for the first time, with his child's first smile, and laughed with her first laugh.

Things with Ivy grew bitter, and as each week went by, and the weeks became months, they argued more and more, battles of vicious words, that poisoned them both.

Years passed, and the fights continued. As Tabitha grew, and began to walk and talk, the young man feared for her, and the effect that her parents might have on her.

Finally, one day, he knew it had to end, and he made a decision as wise as it was foolish. He left. As Tabitha lay sleeping he kissed her goodbye, and walked from the house to the train.

He didn't just leave the house, he left the country. He caught a train, and a boat and another whole series of trains, and one day he got off a ferry in a harbour in a distant land.

A land called Russia.

And if it seems extreme to go all the way to Russia to get away from someone, he knew it was not.

For ivy clings.

Fancy Wooden Box

The young man stepped timidly onto the quayside and looked about him, and breathed Russian air for the first time. Did he know then that that air would never leave him? I think he did. I think he did.

You already know what he carried; a battered leather suitcase in one hand, and a small but sturdy wooden box in the other. He had learnt something already in the course of his journey. If you carry a closed wooden box, people want to know what is in it. All the way across Europe strangers had laid a hand on his shoulder and asked him in a variety of tongues what he was carrying. He thought how funny that was. No one ever asked him what was in his suitcase, though that was every bit as shut as the box. But they could guess. Clothes. Toothbrush and comb. Razor and pyjamas. Tobacco and pipe.

But the box. What the hell was in the box?

Once or twice, he made up something outrageous, just to see their reaction.

A snake. A pair of doves. Pearls and diamonds!

Most of the time, he told the truth, and would even open it to show he wasn't lying.

There. A typewriter. A portable typewriter.

The young man, you see, was a writer.

The typewriter was a marvel of miniaturisation, made from steel and rubber and ivory. A simple enough thing, though to him, a miracle in itself, for in that box was the potential to write everything that could ever be written. Every word, every sentence, every thought that could ever be, was waiting to be made from the machine in the box. Every single idea ever was in there. And that in itself was a wonderful idea.

One day, he thought, I'll write a story about a closed wooden box.

So it was a woman who sent him to Russia.

A woman and fairy tales, both hers, and his.

O, Russia

Arthur. That was the young writer's name.

If I'm to go anywhere, Arthur thought, I'll go to Russia. He may have left Ivy in order to escape her stories, but he came to Russia to find stories of another kind.

Fairy tales.

Like all writers, he had been a reader first, and he thought that Russian fairy tales were the best in the world. People back home didn't know these stories, and he wanted to tell them. They might know Cinderella, and Beauty and the Beast, and Snow White with her raven-black hair, but he thought they ought to know about the Fool of the World, the Little Silver Saucer, and Baba Yaga, the witch, in her hut with chicken legs.

He came to Russia to find these stories, but before he could, he had to learn Russian. He bought a book, one that a Russian child would learn to read from, and he taught himself to read it. And when he had managed that, he picked a harder one, and learned it too, and so on and so on, until one day he picked up a Russian

31

newspaper and read as though it was written in English.

It was a clever thing to do, and his new Russian friends were impressed and amused by it all at once.

Arthur came to the city and found himself a job, and somewhere to live.

He also found himself in the middle of a story beyond anyone's imagination.

Resurrection

The bear sleeps. Somewhere it lies in the darkness of its cave, its heart almost still, its blood crawling through its veins. If you looked from across the sea, from across the country, from just outside the cave even, you would think it was dead, but it truly is only sleeping, waiting for the time to wake.

The time is not yet. Things have to happen first, before the bear can wake. And while the bear sleeps, the Tsar and the Tsarina worry.

True, the Tsar had quashed the trouble threatened by the upstart priest, but now he turned his gaze inwards, inside the palace, to his own family.

His son, Alexei, suffered greatly from his mysterious blood disease. The whole family worried itself sick about the boy, but the effect on the Tsarina was the worst.

At first, she called all the doctors she could find to come and cure her son, Russia's heir. Medical men came from across the city, and from across the whole great country to the palace, and each examined the Tsarevich.

'His veins are too weak,' said one.

'His blood is too thin,' declared another.

But none of them knew what was really wrong. No one knew then that the disease was caused by the blood not thickening when exposed to air. So the doctors prescribed all sorts of quack remedies, but none of them had the slightest effect.

The Tsarina worried. She appointed a sailor, a good strong Russian, loyal, not too young and not too old, to be the boy's protector. The sailor went with Alexei wherever he went, and when the boy was too weak to walk, the sailor carried him.

It was no good, Alexei still managed to hurt himself, as small boys do, and each time there would be an agony of waiting as his body refused to heal itself properly.

Alex, the Tsarina, had had enough. She became convinced that only a miracle from God could save her son, and so, to earn God's favour, she donated large sums of money to the church, and spent hours in prayer.

From time to time she would think her prayers had been answered, as she saw the colour in Alexei's cheeks improve, or watched him playing cards with his sailor, laughing, and happy. But then the illness would return, and snatching Alexei up by the scruff of his neck, would gallop away to the very gates of death.

The Tsarina gave more money to the church, and spent even more hours in fervent prayer, her rich velvet gown growing dusty as she knelt on the cold marble floor in the chapel.

And then, one day, into the royal court walked a monk.

He was wild-looking, and fearsome. He had a long beard, unkempt and dirty, and long matted hair to match. His eyes burned under dark brows. There was a commotion in court and someone ordered that he be thrown out, but the Tsarina raised her hand.

'No,' she said, her heart already willing to give thanks to God. 'Let him speak.'

He said he had walked from Siberia, to come to the palace. He had come to heal the boy, who at that very moment lay perilously ill in bed.

He was taken to Alexei, the Tsarina close behind, the Tsar and his advisors behind them, muttering and prophesying dire consequences.

He sat on the edge of the bed, and the Tsar stepped forward, one hand on his sword, but the Tsarina stopped him with a look.

The monk put his hand on the cover, where Alexei slept fitfully, in a sick peace, and then he opened his eyes.

He sat up, and smiled brightly.

'Hello, Mother,' he said. 'Who are all these people?'

The Tsarina began to weep, and put her hand out to stroke her son's hair. She thanked God in her heart, and then the monk spoke.

'The boy will not die,' he said. 'And when he is thirteen, his disease will be taken from him, forever.'

God's Instrument

Of course, he wasn't a monk at all.

And his religion was not what the Tsar would have called Orthodox. His was a strange mixture of mysticism and sin.

His name was Rasputin, a name he was given as a boy in the village where he grew up, far away, in Western Siberia. Just as other children were called by their nicknames: Clever, Wolf, Big Heart, this dirty scamp took the name meaning 'naughty child'.

The naughty child grew into a vile young man, a drunkard and a lecher. A horse-thief. One day, however, this all changed.

A vision of Mary, the Holy Mother, appeared to him. The apparition said not a word, but he fell on his face in shame and fear. He knew what it meant, and on the spot he repented his wicked ways. Or so he said.

He went on a pilgrimage, to Jerusalem, though he never got there, joining the streams of other holy men and wandering prophets who trailed from one corner of Russia to another, each seeking some hidden goal known only to them.

Until, finally, he walked into this story and into the heart of the Tsarina.

Now the Tsar was more worried than ever.

Rasputin was wild. He was illiterate, he was unwashed and smelt like a goat, and a dirty one at that. He dressed in a peasant's baggy trousers and loose shirt, and his greasy beard was always speckled with bits of food, or crusted soup. His only redeeming feature, it seemed, were his eyes, which could still a room of a hundred voices.

The salons and drawing rooms of the wealthy were already drenched in bizarre practices, occult dabblings, theosophy and spiritualism. Séances were all the rage, the Tsar even suspected the Tsarina had toyed with a ouija board, in an attempt to obtain supernatural aid for her son. And now a wild monk had set up home under his very nose, and there was nothing he could do about it, for Alexandra insisted that God had sent Rasputin to cure their son, as no one else had been able to do.

And even the Tsar had to admit that there was something in it. Whenever the boy grew ill, or hurt himself, Rasputin was called for, and the bleeding would stop, or slow much quicker than usual.

On one occasion, when Rasputin was out of the city, Alexei was injured by a bumpy carriage ride, and a painful tumour grew in his leg. The court doctors told the Tsarina to prepare for the worst; he was going to die. In desperation Alexandra sent a telegram, begging Rasputin to return to the palace. Rasputin did not return, but instead sent a telegram of his own, telling the Tsarina that the tumour would disappear at six thirty that evening.

At six thirty that evening, the tumour disappeared. Rasputin's reputation was sealed, and nothing that the Tsar, or anyone else, could say, would change the Tsarina's mind about him.

Incidences of the Bizarre

Stories twist and turn and grow and meet and give birth to other stories. Here and there, one story touches another, and a familiar character, sometimes the hero, walks over the bridge from one story into another.

This was something that Arthur, the young writer, had learnt. He read his fairy tales in Russian, and saw the same figures pop up here and there, first in this story, then in another. That's why, when he came to write the stories into English, for English children to read, he created three characters who walk through the forest of the whole book, as guardians and guides to every tale. We've met them already. In creating them, they became real, and their names are Peter, the grandfather, and Vanya and Maroosia, his orphaned grandchildren.

As in fairy tale, so in real life, and this is how it was with Arthur too, for he himself was about to walk from one place, and one story, into another.

One day, Russia went to war.

It had been several years since the Tsar last went to war, and it had ended badly that time. But the Tsar's cousin, the Kaiser, had declared war on the countries surrounding his own. So here was another Caesar flexing his muscles, and the Tsar had to send his troops out to stop him.

The Kaiser's men sat in the middle, and the Tsar's armies fought him on the East, and the armies of the Tsar's other cousin, George, on the West. And for years it stayed that way.

The soldiers sat in long holes in the ground, and pointed their rifles over the top from time to time, and sometimes would even try to attack each other, but apart from that nothing very much happened. The soldiers were good soldiers, and did what soldiers usually do, which is to say they made friends with each other, squabbled a bit, got very bored sometimes and very scared other times, and died when they were supposed to.

The young writer knew all about this, and wondered whether he should go and join the soldiers fighting the Kaiser. His brother had already gone, and was somewhere fighting and killing, but Arthur was already in Russia, and had been given an important job, one that meant he didn't have to fight.

Instead, it was his job to report on the war to the people at home, and every day he would find out what he could about what the Tsar's soldiers had been doing, and send a telegram to England, so that people could read about it in their newspapers over breakfast.

But Arthur worried, and decided he needed to talk to a friend, a friend who lived in another city, a day's train journey away.

Nevertheless, he got on a train and went to visit his friend, whose name was Robert. They talked for a long and serious time about the war, and whether Arthur should fight, or whether he should stay and write about it. Arthur found himself wanting to write more fairy tales, but he didn't say anything about that. Instead, he listened to Robert, who was also not a soldier, but had a job that meant he didn't have to fight either. As Acting Consul-General he looked after the British people who lived in Russia, seeing that all their concerns were answered, and that they were safe. He explained to Arthur that some people had to do the sort of jobs that they did, and that it may as well be them as anyone else.

After they had finished talking, Arthur still felt uneasy about it, and to try and cheer him up, Robert suggested they go out. That evening they went to a restaurant, a dining club called the Yar. It was a favourite of Robert's, because it was a gypsy place, and Robert had a great fondness for gypsy songs and dances.

The Yar was wild that night, as wild as ever.

Arthur had never seen anything like it, not even in his young days when he met Ivy, but Robert seemed at ease, and that made Arthur relax too. They had some-

41

thing to eat, and drank a bottle of wine. The restaurant had a large open space between the tables, and here the dancers would whirl and leap, athletic men in shiny black boots and lithe girls with olive skins. Around the sides of the room were cabinets. Small rooms hidden by thick red velvet curtains, where you could dine with a touch more privacy and a great deal more licentiousness. A dancer might be lured into one of these cabinets with the offer of some money, and not reappear for a very long time.

Wine flowed and food was gobbled. Songs were hurled to the rafters, and then a rumour started to buzz around, spreading from one table to the next, whispered by waitresses with wide eyes and loose tongues.

Rasputin was in the restaurant, having walked from one story into another.

By now, his fame had spread far and wide. There were many, many stories about him, about the appalling things he was supposed to have done. He seemed, despite his hideous smell and frightful appearance, to exert some almost hypnotic power, especially over women. It was known that several ladies of the aristocracy had allowed themselves to be debased by him, and his drunkenness and lewdness knew no bounds. He was said to be a great lover, and it was even rumoured that he was having an affair with the Tsarina herself.

Arthur and Robert looked at each other with excitement as they heard the news. Neither of them had ever seen the man in the flesh, and they knew the stories, though there was one story that no one knew, no one outside the palace, that is. Rasputin's miraculous healing of the Tsarevich had been kept secret, known only to the members of the court closest to the Tsar and Tsarina.

A waitress leaned close to Robert and Arthur.

'He's in there,' she hissed, nodding at a curtain on the far side of the room, 'with two men, and three . . .'

Here she leant even closer and whispered even more quietly.

' . . . prostitutki.'

There was a crash of glass and a series of loud shrieks from behind the curtain.

Even the whores had had enough of the beast. The curtain flew open for a second as one of them ran from the restaurant cursing and shouting. The other diners froze, forks halfway to their mouths, as they caught sight for a brief moment of Rasputin, his trousers round his ankles, waving his penis at them.

The curtain swung shut. Police were called, doors continued to bang and swing open. The police arrived, but when they heard who they had been sent to arrest, they refused to do anything. More calls were made, to higher and higher powers, until finally the Chief of Police came. He personally led the absolutely inebriated and docile Rasputin out of the club and away to a prison cell.

The following day however, the Tsar ordered not only the release of Rasputin, but the dismissal of the Chief of Police as well.

Arthur and Robert, like everyone else, were speechless, but then they didn't know the secret of Alexei and his blood. All they saw was the Tsar making inexplicable decisions.

It went like this.

There was blood in the boy, Alexei. Tainted blood.

Only Rasputin could temper the disease, and therefore the Tsarina forgave him anything, because she knew he was a gift from God, and the Tsar could do nothing but agree with the Tsarina's wishes.

'Better Rasputin,' he said, sadly, 'than my wife and child should suffer.'

And Rasputin's word went undisputed.

So when Rasputin told the Tsar that his army would only be victorious if he were at its head, the Tsar left the palace, and went off to the war, leaving Rasputin alone with his wife and child.

And, just then, while the Tsar was far away, the bear began to stir, deep in the darkness of its cave.

It opened one eye, and it was hungry.

Vladimir and Lev, the Russian and the Jew

The bear had forgotten what it felt like to walk through the trees, padding heavily in and out of the silver birches and firs, the snow balling and clumping between his claws. He'd forgotten what it was like to swipe a salmon from the river as the fish leapt upstream to go home to spawn. He'd forgotten what it was like to rub his back against bark, and feel the North wind trying to run its icy fingers through the thickness of his fur.

All he knew was that he was hungry, and that he had to stop this hunger.

He lumbered out of his cave, thinking solemn bear thoughts about food, and made his first stumbling steps out into the winter morning.

The snows were as thick as they had been for five months. Every branch was ice and crystal, and shone with the immaculate beauty of a fast hoarfrost. He remembered now what it was like, the world that he had missed during his hibernation, twelve long years of sleep. Slowly, thoughts and desires crept into his brain, but the hunger in him rose above everything else.

It made him light-headed, and he swayed on his feet as blood began to pump in him as it had done, so many years ago.

Now, only a few trees ahead of him in the forest, stood two men deep in conversation. One was a Russian, the other a Jew, and they were firm friends, though they spent much of their time arguing.

They would argue about all sorts of things, but each would listen politely to what the other had to say. First, the Jew, whose name was Lev, would argue that the people of Russia should be its true masters, and while he did, the Russian, whose name was Vladimir, would stroke his small and excellent beard. Then they would swap, and Vladimir would argue that while what Lev had to say was true, they should not forget that people need guidance from enlightened minds. And Lev would stroke his own small and excellent beard.

Then they'd each light a pipe, and have a good long smoke, while they thought what to argue about next.

The two men, who had both been born in Russia, had since travelled all over the world, and had discussed these questions with many people. There was never silence, wherever they went; there was always talk, talk, talk. Vladimir and Lev had spent the last few years abroad, though in different countries, and at last they were back together in Russia.

It was now, as the Russian and the Jew stood under a tall silver birch at the edge of a clearing, smoking their pipes and stroking their beards, that the bear lumbered into view.

Lev and Vladimir froze, but almost immediately realised that the bear had stopped in its tracks, and showed no sign of attacking them. Very quickly, because both men were very clever, they understood that the bear was confused.

Lev winked at Vladimir, and Vladimir winked back at Lev, because they knew they had found precisely what they'd been looking for. They sauntered over to the bear, each puffing hard on his pipe to hide the fact that they were actually scared, pretending to be as nonchalant as pigs caught in the pantry. Nonetheless, Lev had one hand on the revolver in his pocket. He didn't know how to use it, but it made him feel much better knowing it was there.

'Good Morning, Bear,' Lev said to the animal, who, now that they were up close to it, seemed even bigger.

'Good Morning, Bear,' said Vladimir, but the bear said nothing in reply. Lev and Vladimir looked at each other for a second, then quickly turned back to the bear. It wouldn't do to take your eyes off such a creature for too long.

Lev had an idea. He knew what he should say.

'What's wrong, Bear?' he asked.

The bear answered him.

'I'm hungry,' he declared, in a booming voice that

made the snow tremble from the tops of the trees and flitter down around their shoulders.

'Ah,' said Lev. 'Of course you are. Of course. You're hungry and that's no way for a bear to be. You need food! And maybe you need more than that, too . . . Well, you're in luck, because it just so happens that I, and my friend Vladimir here, are able to help you.'

The bear slowly turned his gaze upon the Russian, who bowed so low that he was brushing the snow off his cap for weeks afterwards.

Then the bear spoke for a second time.

'Indeed,' he said.

'Indeed,' said Lev. 'For why should a creature such as yourself, such a powerful and noble beast, go hungry? You deserve better! You should be the king of the forest, and want for nothing. And why? Because you have been starved. You must rise up, and fight. We will show you how, but you must stand against the man who has taken the food from your mouth!'

'And who is that?' asked the bear, who still seemed a little puzzled.

'Why,' exclaimed Lev, 'the Tsar, of course. He's the one responsible. He has starved the land, and you, the great Russian bear, for too long. He must be swept away! Wipe him from the face of the earth, and you will go hungry no more!'

'The Tsar?' said the bear. 'The Tsar, the Tsar . . . ?'

'Yes,' cried Lev, getting angry himself now, 'the Tsar, and the whole system he controls. A handful of people, unimaginably rich, who have taken everything this country has for themselves, and left you with nothing! Now you must fight to get it back! You must fight.'

Now the bear understood and as he understood he became angry and his hunger only made his anger worse. All the time that Lev had been speaking, Vladimir had sidled out of view of the bear, and had crept around behind him. He'd pulled a frozen but stout branch from a nearby tree, and it had snapped leaving a vicious point on the end. He looked over the bear's shoulder, and with his eyes asked Lev a question.

Lev nodded, ever so slightly, and with that, Vladimir shoved the spike of the branch as hard as he could into the bear's enormous rear end.

The bear howled and shot forward so fast that Lev had to throw himself onto his backside to avoid being trampled there and then. Before he could even get to his feet the bear was out of sight, careering away through the trees.

Vladimir took a couple of steps forward, shouting after it as it went.

'The Tsar! You have to destroy the Tsar! Remember! The Tsar!'

Lev stood up and dusted himself off.

'Well,' he said, 'Do you think that will do it?'

Vladimir nodded.

'Nothing will stop what we have started,' he said,

'because it's been waiting to happen for three hundred years.'

And everything he said was true.

Nothing *would* stop the bear, and that was why, as Grandfather made his way back to the hut to see Vanya and Maroosia and tell them a bedtime fairy tale, the bear bowled out of the trees and ploughed straight towards him.

The old man barely had time to see it coming, and the monster charged him and struck him, sending him flying through the air. The bear knew nothing about it. He was in such a blind rage that he couldn't see, and had just one thing on his mind; one person, the Tsar.

But Vanya and Maroosia heard the noise from inside the hut, and ran out into the snow without even stopping to put their boots on. First they saw a trail of broken branches and undergrowth leading away, and then they saw a dark shape huddled in the snow nearby.

It didn't move.

The children ran over, and knelt by their grandfather.

'Oh Grandfather,' they cried, 'are you all right? Please get up and tell us you are all right.'

But Grandfather said nothing, because he was dead.

Execution

That last tale was a sad one, a very sad one. Once upon a time, more stories had sad endings than happy ones. There was more cruelty casually done than happiness lightly bestowed. Unhappily for Vanya and Maroosia, they were in one of the saddest stories of all.

Now the children had lost not only their parents, but their beloved grandfather too, and as if that wasn't bad enough, the fact was that the bear didn't mean to do it. It was just an accident. Utterly unavoidable, but somehow inevitable, too.

The bear hurtled on through the forest, heading for the Tsar, and Lev and Vladimir followed slowly on behind, in his tracks. They picked their way through the undergrowth of the forest, stopping now and again to refill their pipes, and argue about what they would do when they got to the city.

Even before the bear arrived in the city, another story was reaching an end there. The story of Rasputin.

His behaviour had grown even worse, if that were possible. Not only was he molesting the women of the palace, perhaps even the Tsarina herself, but men as well. And he had engineered the situation so that the Tsar was away at war with the Kaiser. Added to that, suspicion had long ago taken root in many people's minds that the Tsarina, who was German after all, might not want what was best for Russia. Perhaps Rasputin was a spy, sent by the Kaiser, to work with the Tsarina in plotting Russia's downfall.

Unbeknown to him, Rasputin was being watched. Residents of the royal household were under observation at all times of the day, and he was no exception. Police spies drew up long reports. They called them 'staircase notes' but they were spying, all the same.

Eventually, a small group of noblemen came to the decision that they had to act. With the Tsar away, Rasputin had become the Tsarina's key advisor, and it seemed that he was influencing her decisions.

One prince, Felix Yusupov, led the group. He had recently married a beautiful Grand Duchess, but the truth of the matter was that he desired men. Few people knew this outside the court, but while the gorgeous Duchess languished unwanted in her chamber, her husband prowled the murky underworld of the city, looking for excitement. Some say that Rasputin learned of Felix's desires, but when he tried to seduce him, the two men had a violent falling out.

Felix was joined by two Grand Dukes, Dmitri and

Nikolai, and together they plotted Rasputin's end. They thought about it, dark and deadly, and rumours of what they were planning, even the finer details, spread around the city. No one tried to stop them. By some miracle, Rasputin himself seemed unaware of these stories, and so, on the appointed night, he accepted his invitation to the Yusupov palace on the bank of the canal.

A fabulous ball, golden chandeliers and champagne, was in full swing upstairs, or so Rasputin had been told. He had also been told he was going to meet Felix's beautiful wife, Irina, alone. Neither of these things was true. Felix had his servants make the noise of a party upstairs, while he ushered Rasputin in through a side door and down to the basement where Felix had a small suite of rooms he used for private entertaining. Upstairs lay the full splendour of the palace, marble and oak, silk and crystal. Down in the basement, things were much more plain. There were a couple of low-arched rooms, simply furnished. On a small round table lay some refreshments. Some wine, and a few cakes sat on the tablecloth between two candelabra. A fire burned in the grate.

Felix told Rasputin to wait while his wife took leave of her guests, though in reality she was miles away, out of the city. The two Grand Dukes joined them, and they bid Rasputin enjoy the food.

It was such an obvious trap, and yet he walked right into it. The cakes were poisoned, as was the wine. He ate several of the cakes, then drank deeply of the wine, and Prince Felix and his conspirators began to breathe a little more easily.

But an hour passed, maybe longer, and Rasputin showed no sign of illness. Felix grew desperate, and fetching a pistol from his desk upstairs, tricked Rasputin into inspecting a crucifix. While his back was turned, Felix shot him. He fell to the floor with a loud scream, and lay still.

The three conspirators looked at each other and smiled, then went upstairs to dispose of Rasputin's distinctive overcoat, hanging on a hook in the hall. As they reached the ground floor, they heard a commotion from the courtyard. There was Rasputin, crawling on his hands and knees in the snow, shouting. His blood had already left a ghastly red and pink trail in the snow, as he flailed around, trying to find his feet.

He saw them and shouted.

'Felix! I will tell the Tsarina everything, Felix!'

They shot twice and missed.

They shot twice more and hit him. He fell flat.

They kicked him in the head.

They wrapped his body in iron chains and dumped him in the icy waters of the Neva, where two days later it was washed up again.

The murderers were not punished, though Dmitri was exiled, but neither did the murder of Rasputin have the effect they hoped for. They had thought that the

Tsarina, freed from his tyranny, would in turn free the Tsar from his feeble decision-making. Quite the reverse was true, and the Tsar imposed further strictures on his ministers and tried to clamp down even harder than he already had.

There was no happy ending for the murderers, and the Tsar was also approaching the end of his story, because the bear let loose by Lev and Vladimir was on the outskirts of the city.

Miraculous February

The city founded by Peter the Great two hundred years before sat on the river Neva and froze, as if waiting. It was the coldest February anyone could remember; day after day the temperature rose no higher than fifteen degrees below zero. Frost sparkled on the snow like the diamonds that sparkled on the Tsarina's breast.

At the entrance to a block of flats near the beautiful old theatre a porter shook his head in disbelief. He was an old man, and had lived in the city for thirty years, but he'd grown up in Siberia. He tried to cast his mind back to when he was small, wanting to believe that it had been colder in Siberia than it was in the city this February, but he could not. It was cold enough to freeze the thoughts in your head.

He pulled the street door shut with a lazy tug and went back inside to the meagre fire round which his family huddled. They'd run out of coal weeks ago, and it was said there was none to be had anywhere in the city, though the porter wondered if the Tsar and his children were going without coal too. Instead, the porter and his family were slowing burning their house. They'd started on the furniture, and had moved on to the floor. It was remarkable, they'd discovered, how few of your floorboards you actually really needed.

The porter was old, and his hearing was not as good as it had been when he was a boy in Siberia, so he didn't hear a low rumble in the distance. It sounded like thunder, or the cannons of battle, but in fact it was neither of those. It was the bear.

The bear had been travelling for a long time, but far from slowing down, it had if anything speeded up. Something else extraordinary had happened too. As the bear had travelled towards the city it had begun to grow. It got bigger and bigger, until by the time it arrived at the city, the very ice in the river cracked like gunfire beneath its ponderous footsteps. That was the noise the porter hadn't heard.

Then, two astonishing things happened.

First, the sun came out. It came out as if for the very first time, it was so strong. Immediately, the temperature soared to a balmy minus five, and cheered by this, people stuck their noses into the streets as if it were summer. The porter turned to his wife and told her to put the fire out.

'Save the floor for when it gets really cold,' he said, and took one of his coats off to celebrate.

Then, the second remarkable thing happened, and it was even more amazing.

The bear, which by now was as large as the cathedral

on Catherine's canal, rose on its hind legs like a dancing bear in a street market. For a moment the sun was blotted out by its size, and then it fell. As it fell, it came apart. It disintegrated. It fell like brown snow, but each flake was a person. The bear had been one hundred thousand people, and now the people came to earth, tumbling into the snowy streets of the city and picking themselves up, laughing at it all.

Far from being hurt, they realised that they felt strong. But, like the bear, they felt hungry.

They ran through the streets, swarming like bees, joining others who had emerged when the sun had.

It was chaos.

Fights began to break out over nothing, and it was then that Lev and Vladimir arrived.

They'd seen the bear go out of sight over the horizon ahead of them, and had decided to stop talking for a while and get on a train instead, so that they might catch up.

Vladimir and Lev came out of the railway station and found a huge crowd, pressing and heaving on all sides. Lev looked at Vladimir, who nodded. He jumped up onto the bonnet of an armoured car, and with a word, he stilled the crowd.

'Bear!' he cried, and there was silence.

The crowd looked up at him in wonder and expectation. They knew their time had come, and they knew immediately that Vladimir was the man who had given them this time.

'What should we do?' a voice cried.

'Do you not remember? Why did you come here? Do you not remember who it is you've come to see? Who is it who has starved you? Who is it who took you to war, so that the hunger and death got only worse?'

Then the people remembered, and they ran from the station as if someone had shoved a pointed stick up their arse.

'Wait!' called Vladimir after them. 'Wait! The Tsar isn't here, he's at his palace. We need to strike in the city. To remove his puppet ministers! Then we will have power!'

The people were already gone.

Vladimir climbed down from the armoured car, and straightened his cap.

'Do you think they heard me, Lev?'

'Oh, yes,' said Lev, 'I think they heard you. Well, some of them. And as for the rest . . .'

He shrugged.

'It's begun.'

They shook hands and walked into the city that would soon belong to them.

Exit the Fairy Tale, Enter the Storyteller

Now the time for fairy tales is nearly over. But, before they're done, there's time for one more, and, just as all rivers flow into the sea, so that their waters are mixed, all our stories flow together here, into one.

There have been sad stories, as fairy tales often are. It's odd that when people talk about a fairy-tale ending, they mean something good and happy.

There was the story of Vanya and Maroosia, the orphans, who lost their grandfather Peter, killed by a runaway bear. There was the story of the bear itself, and that story is not done yet, not even to this very day.

There was the story of the mad monk, Rasputin, and how his lechery did for him in the end as he drowned in the thick cold waters of the Neva. When his body washed up on the river shore, local women went to drink water from the spot for days afterwards, believing it would contain miraculous healing powers. Even in death his story was not finished. At first his body was embalmed and buried in the palace grounds, but when the bear got there, he dug the body up, and dragged it to the woods in his jaws. There, petrol was poured on it, and it burned. The ashes were thrown to the wind.

There was the story of Alexei and his blood. Exactly how much, ultimately, did that blood have to do with the end of the Tsar? This was truly momentous, for it was not just the end of one Tsar, but of three hundred years of a dynasty, and hundreds more years of other Tsars before them.

Who knows?

Whatever, it was the end for the Tsar. He abdicated, a rather pointless gesture since power would have been taken from him either way. Realising this made the sickly Alexei technically the Tsar, he abdicated for him too. It was all futile.

In the city streets, people confronted troops, the Tsar's soldiers. They faced each other across the thawing snow and the soldiers lowered their rifles to aim at the body of men, women and children opposing them. The soldiers, in their warm uniforms and heavy boots, looked at the people in their rags, many of them bare footed in the snow.

An officer gave the order to fire. No one did.

The officer shouted again, but no one took any notice. Not one of them.

There was a loud cheer from the crowd, and the soldiers cheered back. They shouldered their guns and the two sides walked towards each other, laughing and smiling. The two crowds became one, rifles and caps, jackets and boots were passed from hand to hand until no one could tell who was who anymore. It didn't matter, there was only one side now; the people.

Shots were fired into the air, for joy, and with each shot the people shouted and cheered. They ran riot through the streets, smashing statues of the Tsar, burning his paintings and pulling the all-seeing double-headed eagles from the tops of the gates and doorways. Anything too big to destroy was draped in vast swathes of red cloth. They poured in and out of the buildings once forbidden to them, giddy with their new freedom.

The Tsar, the Tsarina, Olga, Tatiana, Maria, Anastasia and Alexei were all placed under house arrest at their palace and, as they got used to their captivity, they bizarrely enjoyed some of the happiest times of their lives. The Tsar found himself relieved not to have to make decisions any more, and the Tsarina was happy to see her husband more his normal self. The children played through the summer, as they always had, and even young Alexei seemed heartier than usual. It was like one long weekend party, that lasted all summer. The children had their toys, their pets, their books. The difference was that there were guards at every corner, guards who were dressed not in uniform, but in street clothes. The only things that showed they were guards at all were the rifle on their shoulder and a red rag tied as an armband. And they were not unkind, being somehow still in awe of their once so mighty prisoners.

So the Romanovs were happy. For a brief time.

But what of this final story? Well, it's a story about love, and like the others, it flows out to the sea too, to become part of one great tale.

Arthur, the young writer, was tired. He'd been writing about the war; the Tsar's war against the Kaiser, as best as he could, though sometimes he wondered whether anyone was listening. Then he wrote about the new war, the one between the Tsar, and Lev and Vladimir's bear, and still he wondered if anyone was listening. He suffered like everyone else. He was cold and hungry, and then one day he got ill, from something in the water.

He got very, very ill, and nearly died.

When he got well again, he made a decision. He realised how very easy it is to die, and that there were people he needed to see back home before he did anything so drastic.

There was his mother, waiting patiently at home in the Lakes for news of her sons, one fighting in the war, the other writing about it, each in as much danger as the other. He wanted to see her again.

There was Tabitha, his daughter, who would have grown up so much since he had last seen her.

And there was Ivy. He wondered if he'd been wrong about Ivy. They had loved each other once, it was true. Perhaps he'd been too hasty in leaving her. Perhaps there might be something for them after all.

So he caught a train, and a boat and another train and then he visited all the people he wanted to see.

He visited his mother, and he found that he loved her as much as he always did.

He got on another train and went to see Ivy and Tabitha.

He found that he loved Tabitha even more than he always had. To his great delight, he found that she still loved him too. They went for walks together and sang some silly songs and danced down the lane, laughing in the autumn sunshine.

Things in fairy tales come in threes, that was something else that Arthur had learnt as a reader and a writer. Two things go this way, the third goes that. Two things are good, the third is bad.

So maybe he wasn't surprised to find that when he went to see if he still loved Ivy, he found that he did not.

For three days, they fought and wrestled, and he knew it was time to leave again, though he knew that if he left Ivy, he would perhaps lose Tabitha too.

But it had to be.

He kissed Tabitha's sleeping head once more, crept from the house, and with a broken heart he caught a train early one morning.

A few days later he caught another train, and then a boat, and then yet another train, and he came back to that great city where history was churning out more stories than could ever be written down.

It was Christmas Day.

A lot had happened since he'd left.

The people, who now called themselves Reds, had decided that they enjoyed what had happened in February so much, that in October they did it all again.

Things had not moved on as much as they had hoped and desired, and some people were even suggesting that the Tsar should be returned to power. In response, the last trace of the Tsar's government was swept away, and anyone who disagreed was swept aside with it.

Arthur realised he had missed the biggest story of his life and that he had to do something about it. He spent the next couple of days chasing round the city, looking for stories to write down and send back home.

It seemed to him that the vital thing was to talk to the people in charge, and he soon learned that their names were Lev and Vladimir.

He couldn't find Vladimir at all. But a day or so before the year ended, he found Lev in a huge old building that had been a school for rich girls until the coming of the bear had frightened them all away. The school was so big that Lev and his friends decided that the best way to get round it was by bicycle.

Arthur wandered through cavernous corridors, open mouthed. It was an unusual sight; the building was magnificent, or rather it had been, but its new inhabitants seemed not to care for the richness of the place. It was a mess. Litter lay everywhere. Cigarette ends had been trodden into the carpets, paintings lay slashed on the floor.

Oh, thought Arthur, so the mighty have fallen!

Finally, at the end of a long corridor on the first floor, he found the door he had been looking for.

It was number 67, and on a piece of paper stuck to the door with a drawing pin was Lev's name.

Arthur knocked, but there was no reply. He knocked louder, but still there was no reply. The third time, he thumped the door so hard the paper trembled, and the door swung open.

There was a room full of people, all busy, all talking. No one had heard him knocking, and no one seemed to take any notice of him, so he tugged someone's sleeve.

'Lev?' he asked.

The man shook his head, and pointed at a further door.

'In there,' he said. 'He's expecting you.'

Arthur made his way across the room, round piles of papers and piles of rubbish, and put his hand on the brass doorknob. As he did so, he saw that he was being watched by a woman, and had to turn away, because she was too beautiful to look at.

He opened the door, and let himself in, and there was Lev, deep in conversation on the telephone. He motioned for Arthur to come in.

He finished his phone call, though he took his time, but then Arthur and he talked, and Arthur made notes in his head for the story he would write later.

Arthur was very impressed with Lev, and saw that he was a clever man, which he could tell from the way he stroked his small and excellent beard when he was thinking.

Arthur left, and on his way through the outer room, was disappointed and relieved to see that the beautiful woman had gone, but as he made his way down the stairs, he saw her on the landing. He felt his eyes pull to hers, then look away, but not before he had seen her smile, ever so slightly.

It was night time. Arthur had spent the afternoon in his flat writing up his stories, but now he slipped into his old greatcoat, and as he ventured outside again, he was assaulted by the brutally low temperature.

Snow lay across the city's roads, swept by the wind into fantastical shapes and then frozen hard by the imperious cold. Arthur was weary, and hungry too, but his work was not yet done for the day. He had to send his stories back home, and to do that meant asking permission from the censor who was in charge of such matters.

On foot, he made his way slowly across the city to where this man worked, and found no guard on the door. It was late and the building was deserted, so he walked the empty corridors, calling out now and again for anyone who might hear.

Finally, he saw light coming from under a door ahead of him. Thinking it had to be the man he had come to see, to approve his stories, he opened the door.

There inside, was what he had been looking for.

Not the man he needed, but something else entirely.

A woman stood with her back to him, bent over something he could not see. She turned and he saw it was the beautiful girl from the school. Light from a single candle lit her face softly, and she smiled.

In one hand she held a wooden spoon, and now he saw that she had been stirring something in a pot over a small stove.

Arthur stepped into the room, and waved his stories.

'Do you know where the censor is?'

The girl shook her head. Her short dark hair swung, half-covering one lovely eye. She held the spoon delicately, as if it were some kind of magic wand.

'This is what you want,' she said, almost in a whisper.

She nodded at the pot, and Arthur found himself drawn towards her. He looked inside.

'Potatoes,' she murmured, as if it were the most beautiful word in the world. Her eyes lit up and Arthur realised how very hungry he was. He stood no more than a weak moment's decision away from her, and looked into her eyes.

This is what you want.

And that was how the young writer found love, just when he had stopped looking for it.

Darkness into Daylight

The world was changing. Nothing could stop that. There can be no magic by daylight, it is a thing of the dark and shadows and the black and white of night time, and just as that is true, it is also true that fairy tales cannot live in the modern world of colour.

The time for princes and tsars and grand duchesses and especially holy madmen was gone. In its place came a world of war and revolution, of tanks and telephones, of murder and assassination.

The bear had already become what it had been waiting to be, and the men who set it on its journey changed too. Lev became Trotsky, Vladimir took the name Lenin, and they stepped into a bright and furious modern world; blood red, and snow white.

Part Two

One Night in Moscow

Ночь в Москве

Before

Twelve hundred feet above the Baltic sea it is dark and cold. The sun is eclipsed by a huge bank of snow clouds that are about to birth themselves over the Russian coastline. The snow falls, but slowly, flickering its way from the heavens down towards the ground, and the city.

Petrograd. 1917.

Three years ago, on the outbreak of war with the Kaiser, the noble city of St Petersburg changed its name to something less German sounding. Now with a good Slavic name, the city is changing again, but this time something more important than a name is at stake. It's a city struggling to break free of the past; like the snow clouds, it's about to give birth to something new, a new version of itself, modern and clever. But, like a calf stuck in knee-deep mud, the going is difficult.

It is only late afternoon, but already it's dusk. Shadows spread, along the wide, wide streets, and narrow alleys alike. People, grey people, flit like sewer rats, gone as soon as they're seen, each with some dreadful history of their own to take part in. There's a man who strangled his neighbour for a piece of mouldy bread; there's a woman who left her crying baby in a bundle by the river because she could not feed it.

A few fires smoulder at street corners, other figures hunched around them, silent and blind. The city seems deserted, but it's not. There is life; there are people, but they're out of sight, in once beautiful halls, talking about the life and death of a nation.

Having left one of these meetings, a young Englishman called Arthur makes his way home across the breadth of the city, from the Tauride Palace in the East, to his flat in Glinka Street in the West. Though he is English he is no stranger to the city and knows it well, from the gaudy domes of the Church of our Saviour on Spilled Blood, to the brooding mass of the Peter and Paul Fortress in the river, from the newly built Astoria Hotel to the Summer Garden.

His way takes him down some of the most impressive streets in Petrograd, but now even these broad avenues are dwarfed by the painful emptiness of a square so big he can barely see the far side. The Champ de Mars.

It's here the snowflakes hit first, joining their dead relations already lying in the square, where, with no sun to shine and make it sparkle, the snow forms a dull white blanket across the city. It's here, too, that one flake lands by an extraordinary chance on the barrel of a revolver. The revolver is held in the hand of a cavalry-man, riding his horse hard across the square.

Arthur is caught by the sight of the solitary horseman and stops in his tracks. He watches the rider for a few more seconds, when it occurs to him that man and beast are heading in his direction.

'No,' he says aloud, 'no one's interested in me,' though there's not a soul to hear. But talking helps to keep him warm, or keep his mind off the cold, at least. He sets off again, and as he moves, he sees the horseman change direction, steering towards him. There is no mistake.

The horse covers the last few yards in a flurry of hoof and flying snow, and comes skidding to a halt.

Arthur opens his mouth, but before he can speak, finds himself staring at the mouth of a gun.

He freezes, and does precisely nothing, during which time he sees beyond the barrel of the gun the sharply trimmed moustache on the cavalryman's face. He notices the fine braid on his regimental greatcoat, the snow unmelted on his fur hat, and likewise the snow unmelted on the barrel of the revolver.

The rider waves the gun a fraction, staring at Arthur as if he has the keys to the world. Then, his horse pulling beneath him, he shouts.

'For the people, or against the people?'

Arthur stares back from under his own fur hat, his own greatcoat feeling as thin and useless as gossamer, faced with the prospect of a bullet. He opens his mouth again, and this time some words came out, though they're not of his control.

'I am English,' he says.

The horseman looks at Arthur intently, hesitating. The tip of the gun lifts towards the Englishman's head slightly and he closes his eyes.

'Long live England!'

The rider laughs and puts his gun away.

'Long live England,' he shouts, salutes, then gallops away across the snow.

Arthur starts to breathe again. He pulls the brim of his hat down a little further against the snow, and makes his way across to the far side of the Champ de Mars. He smiles.

3.45 p.m.

A year and a half has passed.

Arthur is walking home again, but home is not in Glinka Street anymore. He is not even in Petrograd now, but Moscow. He has taken a room in the only hotel open to the public, the Elite, where a hotch-potch of foreigners like him are clinging to whatever it was that brought them to Russia in the first place.

A lot has happened in eighteen months, and as he pushes through the doors into the lobby, he does not smile.

He keeps his head down, but there they are as usual; the doorman and a girl of about nine who always hangs around him; his daughter, Kashka.

The doorman has many children. His eldest son is away in the army somewhere, and the girl is the youngest of five. As usual, the doorman nods suspiciously at the young foreigner, and as usual the girl smiles and waves at him. Then she asks her question, as she always does.

'Please, sir. When will the war end?'

Why she asks him and not her father, he has no idea.

Maybe it is something to do with being foreign, with being English. The Russians see the English as rulers of the world, and as allies. Together they have been fighting the same war against Germany for four years. It's Arthur's belief that England can help Russia see her way through the Revolution and remain strong. If Russia stays strong, he has always believed, she will be able to help fight Germany, and then the war might end sooner. And then Geoff might come home, and their mother will have her sons back, safe and sound. And the doorman's daughter might get her big brother back too.

He looks over to where she stands on the threshold of the doorman's tiny office, and gives the answer he always gives.

'Soon, Kashka, soon.'

Through his articles for the *Daily News* he's been working hard to get England to understand Russia better. Or had been, but everything changes eventually. Everything.

He looks at his pocket watch.

Four in the afternoon. He has six hours left.

He pads up the stairwell, once opulent but now filthy and uncared for, and down the corridor on the second floor to his room.

He fumbles briefly for the key in his pocket and is about to unlock the door when he stops himself and remembers what he's supposed to do. He checks the door jamb for the tiny slip of paper he put there when he left.

It's still in place.

'Robert, you worry too much,' he says, thinking of his friend, but he's still not smiling. He pushes into his room, barely tidier than the city itself, and collapses on the bed, where, without even taking his boots off, he wastes one whole delicious hour in sleep.

4.30 p.m.

Though his body rests, his mind does not, and tortures him.

The unsettled streets of the city only serve to heighten his unsettled nerves, and bring back all sorts of memories. Bad memories.

He has often wondered why it is that some things stay with you and others do not. There are moments from his life, from as far back as early childhood, that he can see as if they happened yesterday.

A fishing trip with his father, rambling in the hills over Coniston, swimming in the Duddon. Being taught to ice-skate at the age of four by a Russian prince. Kropotkin, that was his name. How could you forget a name like that? The very same Kropotkin who is now an elderly anarchist. Arthur has met him once, Prince Anarchy, but was unable to see the man he met at the age of four. Nevertheless, there was still kindness in his eyes.

And then there are things that stay with you for a

different reason, things you wish you could wash from your mind, but, like blood, are hard to wash out. The screams of a wounded hare his father had shot on a hunt; its unearthly shrieks rang in his ears for days, it seemed. Now it appears that among all the horrors he has witnessed since the Revolution began, one is going to haunt his dreams for the rest of his life.

He'd seen bad things before. He'd made several trips to the Russian front to report for the *News*, and had seen men half-dead, the reek of decay already on them, as some wound or other festered and stank beneath dirty bandages.

When the Revolution happened, that February in Petrograd, he'd had a ringside seat. He'd been swept along by the thrill of it all, like the rest of the city. The surge of new-found freedom was infectious; the air was filled with a spirit of togetherness which was hard to ignore. There was fighting, of course, though what Arthur had seen was more chaotic than dangerous.

Nevertheless, he'd dodged falling grenades, and stooped beneath the whistle of hapless rifle fire, all issuing from unseen assailants fighting on unknown orders.

He'd watched from the window of his flat one grey and snowy afternoon and seen the Revolution, or one part of it at least, take place before his very eyes. There'd been sporadic shooting in the square outside the Mariinsky Theatre all day. Anyone caught out in the open had rushed across, trying to duck under the bullets, running with their arms around their heads as if being chased by bees.

Still, Arthur hadn't stopped to think of the danger, either to himself or to anyone else. The porter told him there was a police machine gun on the roof of the theatre, and another on their own roof too. These were answered by rifle shots from revolutionaries hidden in surrounding buildings; their target not the theatre, but the building that lay beyond it across the canal; the Litovsky Castle. Inside, soldiers from the Lithuanian Regiment, still faithful to the Tsar, were under siege.

Arthur watched from the window, notebook in hand, until after an hour or two of stand off, a postal car hurtled into view round the corner of Glinka Street. It careered wildly across the snow, but the driver expertly skidded to a stop. The small yellow motor van sported a large red flag, that looked to be silk. That was typical of a revolutionary. Now its purpose became clear, as the car swung round and Arthur saw a machine gun lying propped up in the rear. Two men hauled the beast around and a third fed it a huge belt of ammunition. It began to vomit bullets towards the castle, a grim-looking building with squat round towers at its front.

The machine-gun fire from the car was answered by a stuttering noise from the roof above Arthur's head and now he knew the porter had not been lying. Sensing the danger, the driver of the car sped away again, out of sight behind the far side of the theatre. As it went, the men in the back sprayed shots aimlessly. There was a loud triple crack by Arthur's head and he fell backwards. Dazed, he got to his feet to see the glass of his window still intact, though bullets had obviously raked the stone work right outside.

The firefight continued all afternoon, until, in the early evening, with the castle burning, the soldiers inside gave themselves up.

Arthur scribbled notes for the newspaper, keeping one eye on the square below him. His heart pounded from the fright of the near miss, but he felt exhilarated, and a kind of fearlessness came into him. He pulled on his greatcoat, a souvenir he'd picked up on a trip to the front; once a Tsarist officer's. To avoid misunderstandings, he'd cut off all the insignia and braids, and was left with a superbly warm garment that despite his height swept right down to his ankles. Shoving his fur hat on his head, he made his way out into the new revolutionary world, hungry for a story. This was the front line of history, here, now, and it made his blood beat to think of it.

He walked north up Glinka Street towards the bridge over the canal, and across the water saw a group of revolutionary soldiers. They were at ease, and Arthur smiled to see them laughing and joking, gently punching each other's shoulders, as if oblivious of any danger. Arthur crossed the bridge, thinking to interview them, when he saw another figure in the middle of the group. From his uniform, Arthur could see he was an officer, and now he understood. A street door banged in the wind. The officer had been dragged outside. The soldiers were pushing him from one to another, as if playing a schoolyard game. They laughed again.

Arthur was halfway across the bridge, when they pushed the officer out to the edge of the quayside. He obviously knew what was expected of him, for he made no attempt to run. One of the revolutionaries stepped forward and lifted his arm as if pointing at the Tsarist.

There was a bang, and at the same moment, the top of the officer's head disappeared in a cloud of red pulp. The revolutionary dropped his arm and cordite smoked from the barrel of his pistol into the February dusk.

The thrill that had been coursing through Arthur's blood died as the soldier did, and he thought he was going to be sick. He stood there for an age, unaware that the revolutionaries had spotted him and were shouting at him. Somehow, the fact that he seemed to be ignoring them worked in his favour.

They got bored and wandered off.

Eventually, Arthur found his way home, went to sleep, and had the nightmare that he's having again today, where, with infinite slowness, he watches the officer's brains float away in the wind like a red mist, across the canal, and out to the bay.

5.05 p.m.

Arthur wakes from his sleep. He rolls onto his side and swings his feet to the floor, rubbing his eyes with the back of his hand.

Five past five. Under five hours left. Then he has to go and meet Robert, and by then it will be too late to change his mind.

He goes to the window. Outside, is a rare sight. Moscow in the sunshine. When it's hot in Russia, it's very hot; it's just that he's discovered that the winter lasts for nine months and the other three seasons fight it out for the rest.

Snow is always in his mind. So much of everything he can remember about his life in Russia is painted on a backdrop of snow, and a cold that's hard to imagine unless you've felt it yourself. At the Galician front one winter he saw soldiers frozen solid where they stood, like pale white statues that might, against the odds, return to life at any moment. None of them ever did.

He's formed the opinion that little can have changed in warfare since Napoleon tried to capture Moscow. The great French General was beaten by the winter rather than the Russian army. Napoleon, the master tactician, should have known better, but no one seems to have learnt from the lesson, and from what Arthur can tell the cold and hunger is killing more Russian soldiers than the war ever has.

Even in the heat of July, snow is never far from Arthur's mind. How wonderful it would be to be cool! Last winter, when the hunger was at its worst in the city, he took his rod to the Neva and joined the others fishing through holes in the ice. He caught enough one day to feed a family, which is exactly what he did, giving all but one perch to the porter. The porter had said nothing, but later, his wife had come upstairs and hugged Arthur, tears running freely down her face.

He turns from the window, scratching his head.

What to do with the time he has to spare? Certainly, it would not do to think too much. He has made up his mind, and cannot go back on it. Robert Bruce Lockhart, the closest thing to a friend he has left in Russia, is a very persuasive man.

Once, there were dozens of other Englishmen in the city. Journalists like himself mostly, men from the *Telegraph*, the *Manchester Guardian*, the *Times*, Reuters. They had welcomed him as a colleague when he arrived for the *Daily News*, though he knew nothing about being a journalist at the time. They'd had to show him the ropes, even down to how to write in telegraph language, using as few words as possible where every one cost a kopek.

He may have known little about journalism, but he was a writer, and he had one advantage over the other journalists; he knew Russian, having taught himself from Russian children's books, working his way up to newspapers in three months flat.

Now, they're all gone. All the journalists, and even his friend Will who'd worked for the Russian government under the old regime until his job had disappeared one day when revolutionaries stormed their offices. Will left even before the second Revolution, in October, when the Bolsheviks rose to power under Lenin and Trotsky.

Arthur decides what to do. He will do the most important thing in the world. He sits down at his desk and pulls out some paper, and three bottles of ink. The black, that he always uses, is getting low, but today he pulls out a bottle of red and a bottle of green that he saves for the most special letters, to Tabitha.

He writes a long letter to his daughter, using the coloured inks to draw silly pictures, ones that he knows will make her laugh, and he ends by asking her if she's read the book he wrote yet. A book called *Old Peter's*

Russian Tales, about an ancient but kindly Russian woodcutter and his two orphaned grandchildren, Vanya and Maroosia, who live in a hut in the middle of a hundred thousand snow laden fir trees.

5.40 p.m.

Letter written, Arthur spends a careful five minutes folding the paper neatly and sealing the envelope; writing the address as clearly as he can. It has become something of a ritual, as though, by taking immaculate care in the preparation of his letters, it will somehow protect them on their journey to England.

It was on his last visit home that he realised how few of his letters actually got through.

'Do you ever hear from that brother of mine?' he'd asked his mother one evening, and she'd showed him a shoebox where she kept letters from both her sons; Arthur in Russia, Geoffrey in France.

Arthur gazed at the few letters knocking around in the bottom of the box.

'He writes as often as he can,' his mother said as if justifying something. She smiled. 'Just as often as you do.'

'But I've written countless letters. One a week, sometimes more. For years. There must be more than this.'

He picked up a letter, and marvelled at it. There was

his own handwriting, put on the envelope in Petrograd, and somehow the fragile little thing had made its way across Europe with less trouble than Arthur and a dozen trains and boats had. Others though, it seemed, had not been so lucky.

That evening, he sat in the drawing room and listened to the sound of the geese calling to fly south, leaving the hills and lakes for another winter, while his mother cooked in the kitchen. He went through the letters that had survived, and as he read, he began to wonder if there was some pattern, to which had survived and which had not. Letters where he spoke of mundane things, of friends and family, were, by and large, safe. But he could remember other letters where he'd written of the war, of the Revolution, of politics and Bolshevism, and it seemed to him that more of those were missing.

He inspected the envelopes of the letters with which he was now reunited. Had they been opened twice?

It was hard to tell.

Arthur looks at his watch again, then throws the letter to Tabitha on the bed. He'll take it to the post office when he goes out later. He looks at it sadly, because he knows there's another barrier for that letter to cross, and this time not some unseen governmental hand, but one that belongs to a woman he knows all too well.

Tabitha's mother.

6.00 p.m.

One night in Moscow.

That's all it's come down to now. Just a few hours left before he'll go and meet Lockhart, and yet, this single brief evening could last a week, a month, or a year. As his mind drifts, the evening expands to encompass all the years he's spent in Russia, all the people he's ever met. Miserably, he wonders if there will be a future after this evening, one in which he might have a chance to live and to love, but then he berates himself. He has no right to feel miserable; the time for feeling anything has passed.

Now, it's time to act.

If only there weren't so many hours to kill. Four long hours.

When did it all start?

It's hard to be sure. He wanders round his room, remembering the episode with his mother and the letters. He'd had a clue about things then, but he supposed it went way back before that. Maybe it had started when he'd met Lockhart for the first time, nearly three years ago. Lockhart had been posted to Moscow, and was dropped in at the deep end when the Consul-General went home to England suffering from ill health. Lockhart had been made Acting Consul-General, a younger man even than Arthur. They'd become friends immediately, though so different in nature. Robert, the Scot, practical, wise and yet passionate too, Arthur felt so intimidated by his confidence, by his knowledge. In Lockhart's presence he had quickly realised how naive he was.

Maybe it had started then, as Lockhart had opened his eyes to the reality that not everyone is what they seem.

Or maybe it had started even before that, with the British Ambassador, Buchanan.

Arthur remembers one of their first meetings, long before the Revolution. As a British journalist, he naturally spent some time every day at the Embassy, up on the Neva embankment, gathering what news there was to be had.

He'd got talking to Buchanan, an old-school gentleman with a neat grey beard. Arthur worried that he was shirking his duty as an Englishman.

'My brother Geoff is in France,' he explained, 'yet I'm here in the safety of the British Embassy talking to you. Shouldn't I go and fight?'

Buchanan smiled.

'You don't look like the fighting type,' he said.

'Who does?' Arthur said, and Buchanan conceded the point.

'Some do, I suppose. Many do not. And besides, there are other ways of fighting. You may come to be more use to Britain here than getting yourself killed in France. Did you hear the news about Ypres? I mean the real stuff, not what your lot print in your papers. All in all I think you can do more good here.'

'You mean as a journalist?'

There was a slight pause during which Buchanan seemed to be weighing something up.

'Yes, that,' he muttered at last.

A year on he'd gone to see Buchanan to ask for help.

'I'm off home. To England I mean.'

'What of it?'

'When I come back . . . The journey may not be as easy as last time. And even then it was damn hard.'

'What can we do?' said Buchanan.

'Have I ever shown you this?' Arthur asked, and pulled a folded and somewhat crumpled letter from his pocket. He handed it to Buchanan and was amused by the look of bewilderment that spread across the Ambassador's face.

'This is all very interesting, Ransome,' he said, some of his customary charm slipping slightly. 'But why are you showing me a letter written to you by the Imperial Lending Library of London, declaring that you have five books heavily overdue?'

93

'That letter,' Arthur said, 'has helped me out of more sticky situations than I can tell you.'

Buchanan raised an eyebrow.

'Last year I was stuck at the Romanian border, and I started waving that about; it got me through. Same thing in Finland, Galicia and Russia. Anywhere they can't read English. Passports and visas are all very well, but pull something mystifying like that out of your pocket and it can work wonders.'

A slow but gratifying smile spread across the Ambassador's face.

'It does have rather a splendid crest, doesn't it?'

'Yes, sir. Embossed too, you'll notice. Terrifying type-face. I think that and the one word they can read; London, is enough.'

'So what you're saying is that you'd like me to write you a genuine version, a sort of passepartout.'

'That's the idea.'

'Something like this?'

Now it was Arthur's turn to feel baffled as Buchanan pushed an envelope across the leather of the desk. The envelope was not sealed and Arthur slid out a letter written on Embassy headed notepaper, thick and crisp.

He read it and swiftly held up his hand, acknowl-edging he had been trumped.

'Thank you, sir.'

'Anything else?'

'No . . . well, yes,' he said, indicating the letter. 'But

how did you know I'm heading . . . '

'Do you think there are any secrets in this city, Ransome?'

Arthur shook his head, as much in puzzlement as agreement.

'And this part here?' he said, looking at the last line. 'What of it?'

'I've assisted the Embassy for three years . . . ?'

'Well?'

'That's not strictly true, sir.'

'No, Ransome, but it's not strictly untrue, is it? Oh and one more thing. Stop using that fool letter from the library. You'll get yourself shot.'

No secrets in the city.

Slowly he had learned that there is a world beneath the visible one, and that people, some people at least, have a different life, that they carry inside them. Maybe if he'd been less innocent he would have seen earlier what was going on.

On the way back from England, after that short visit home, they'd already begun to make use of him, and once they've used you once, they think you're theirs.

The journey from England to Russia, always a tortuous one, was made even harder by the fact that the Bolsheviks were now ruling Russia.

Before leaving London he'd had to get a permit to

travel from the Foreign Office. An interview there with Lord Cecil was educational; he thought the chances of getting back to Russia were slim.

Arthur opened his mouth to protest, but Cecil raised a hand to stop him.

'Oh, we'll give you your permit, Ransome,' he said. 'Don't worry about that. I mean simply that you may find it hard to convince the Bolsheviks to let you back in. Unless you know differently?'

Arthur didn't really register this last remark, and merely thanked him for the permit.

'But we'll do better than that,' Cecil replied. 'Something that can get you as far as Stockholm without question. I have a bag, a diplomatic bag, that needs delivering to Sir Esmé Howard, our man there. If you undertake to carry it you'll be guaranteed safe passage under diplomatic immunity. Do we have a deal?'

Arthur thought for a moment, but could see no point in refusing. Besides, he had read and written enough fairy tales to know that things come in threes. With this latest addition he would have three talismans to keep him safe; his letter from Buchanan, his permit from the Foreign Office, and Cecil's bag. Enough to see him past three trolls, three dragons, or three witches, at least.

Cecil's word was true. The bag got Arthur as far as Stockholm, but then he got stuck. Cecil had been right about the Bolsheviks, too. They refused him a visa to return to Petrograd. It was something of his own making that saved him.

6.00 p.m. continued

Arthur rolled and rattled across Northern Europe in boats and trains; typewriter on one side, suitcase on the other, and now, a third bag, a slim leather briefcase, clutched in his lap.

He saw people looking at his typewriter box, and now he knew what it felt like, for he was every bit as curious about what was in the diplomatic bag on his lap.

At the British Embassy in Stockholm he waited for an hour for the minister to meet him, and then, with a brief nod, Sir Esmé took the briefcase and was gone, without a word. Arthur stood about feeling like an idiot, then slunk outside, wondering what the hell had been in the bag. A letter from the pompous old man's mother? Some dreadful novel perhaps? Both of those seemed unlikely. State secrets? If that were so, just what did that make him?

He spent the next three days walking from one end of Stockholm to the other, trying to find out who he needed to talk to, to get back into Russia. It was a gilded cage affair. He didn't see the beauty of the wonderful old city spread across dozens of islands, like a fleet of floating buildings, and he didn't see the beauty of the buildings themselves, or the pretty Swedish girls who served him breakfast at the hotel. He knew he had to get back to Russia, to get on with his job, and that was all he could think about.

At last he discovered that he needed to get permission from the Bolshevik emissary to Sweden, a man named Vorovsky, but Vorovsky flatly refused to see him. He persisted for another couple of days, and still got nowhere, but then one day there was a note waiting for him at his hotel.

It was from Sir Esmé, and apparently Arthur was to join him for lunch the following day.

Somewhat mystified, Arthur presented himself at the Embassy at the appointed hour, wondering what trouble he was in now. He hadn't touched the contents of the bag; they were sealed and he'd not even so much as thought about breaking the seal, not seriously.

He was shown into a sumptuous dining room where a feast lay spread. Sir Esmé was waiting for him, and this time he was smiling.

'Ransome!' he declared, as if Arthur had returned from the moon. 'Good of you to come. I'm so very glad you're still in Stockholm.'

Behind the minister, two children stood nervously peeking out from behind his back, a boy and a girl, both more or less Tabitha's age, he thought.

Arthur began to wonder what was going on, but Sir Esmé was talking again.

'Why on earth didn't you say who you were, man?'

'But I did, I . . .'

'I mean the book. Why didn't you say you were *that* Ransome?'

Something began to dawn on Arthur, and he smiled.

'I didn't think . . . I mean why would you be . . . '

'Well, never mind. I'm just relieved you haven't left. When I mentioned your name at supper the night before last I was nearly lynched by these two!'

He turned to his children.

'Isn't that right?'

They giggled.

'Children! Meet Mr Arthur Ransome.'

Now Arthur knew what to do; he was on familiar ground. He bowed low and solemnly, and then straightened, winking at them.

'They're big fans of yours, you see,' Sir Esmé said. 'So won't you join us for some lunch?'

Arthur smiled at the children.

'Well now,' he said. 'You must be Maroosia, and you must be Vanya, yes?'

They squealed with delight, and then all four sat down to eat.

Arthur stayed all afternoon, and earned his keep by

telling stories, lots of stories, ones there l
room for in the book, and other ones en
Africa and India. But it was the Russian s
liked the best.

By the end of the afternoon, he left behind
two happy children and came away with a letter of
introduction from the minister to Vorovsky, and three
days later, got his visa to return to Petrograd.

6.10 p.m.

Arthur realises the post office will be shut long before he's due to meet Lockhart, and with a sigh puts his light summer jacket on again. His shoulders ache as he pulls it on, and he wonders how he got like this. He's still young, so why is it that he feels like a very old man?

His hand is on the doorknob when he hears a noise outside in the corridor. He freezes, holding his breath, straining to hear. Nothing. But he waits anyway, makes himself count to a minute before he dares move.

Then, there it is again. A faint scuffling sound somewhere close outside.

Inch by inch, Arthur bends over to peer through the keyhole, only to discover that with the key still in it he can see almost nothing.

The noise comes again and he can bear it no more; he whips the door open and bursts out not knowing what he will do if there is a Cheka agent brandishing a gun, only to find an old man leaning against the wall. It's a neighbour from along the corridor. He looks at Arthur, bemused, but smiles.

'These stairs will kill me one day, I swear to God!'

He sighs, and having caught his breath, shuffles off down the corridor.

Arthur shakes his head.

It's not far to the post office, even though the Bolsheviks have moved it from its old home. He scurries along the Moscow streets, with high pavements and dirt roads. The ancient capital is somehow less stark than Petrograd; maybe it's the architecture. Petrograd, barely two hundred years old, was built to a formal plan as stipulated by Peter the Great; Moscow has grown organically and as a result is less regimented, less imposing somehow. Maybe it's to do with buildings, but Lockhart says it's the people who make Moscow more welcoming. Arthur doesn't agree and anyway, he thinks it as odious to compare them as it would be to compare one man's wife with another's.

He looks at his watch and hurries on; the post office is supposed to stay open until half past six, but there's never any guarantee in Russia that people will stick to the appointed times.

Damn you, Lockhart.

The words run through his mind and as soon as they do he tries to push them away. He's made his decision, he can't go back on it. He can't let Robert down.

Yes, he thinks, as he joins the queue in the post office, it was Lockhart who got him into all this, though certainly Buchanan had started the ball rolling even before the Scot turned up in Petrograd.

And then again, there were those damn Russians; the Bolsheviks. They're so infuriating *en masse*, and yet individually, they're the most charismatic and likeable men Arthur has ever met.

He remembers his first visit to the Smolny Institute in Petrograd, the old girl's school, to interview Trotsky, who at the time was effectively the dictator of the whole new Russia. He wandered down corridor after corridor until finally he found his way to the door marked '67'.

Even then suspicion tapped at the edge of his mind. When he'd arrived, to talk to Trotsky, he'd been told he was expected.

Expected? Why was he expected? How did anyone, let alone Trotsky, know about him?

That would have been his first question, but he knew he wouldn't have long with the powerful man, so instead he asked the question his newspaper would want him to ask; what was Trotsky going to do about the war with Germany? Were they going to keep fighting as Britain wanted, or surrender to the Kaiser and ask for peace terms?

They talked, or rather, Trotsky talked, and Arthur listened. Trotsky held forth eloquently for fifteen minutes without pause, during which time Arthur absorbed the details of the room. It was almost Spartan.

A simple dark polished wooden floor, a single desk, three chairs. In the corner of the room was an armchair and standard lamp. On the desk was a table lamp matching the other, and a telephone. An inkwell, three piles of papers. That was about it, though Arthur also noted a small neat hole, a bullet hole, in one of the windows.

Such a small thing, but it shook him, reminding him who he was talking to, and what was at stake.

Trotsky's position on Germany was a simple one. Arthur asked him how he was going to get decent peace terms from Germany if he surrendered to them; it was obvious that Germany would take as much land and resources from Russia as she chose if this were to happen. Trotsky's answer was that the German people themselves, the workers, would rise and force their own government to feel the pressure of democracy, just as had happened in Russia. He was totally confident of this and Arthur was struck by the steel in his eyes, softened by the expressiveness of his mouth. He felt overawed. Why were there some people who seemed so sure of themselves that it made him feel small and ignorant by comparison, as if they had a script to life with all the answers on it? He felt he didn't even know the questions.

With an abrupt wave of his hand, Trotsky indicated the interview was over, and Arthur stood. As he turned to go, however, curiosity got the better of him.

'How did that get there?' he asked, nodding towards the bullet hole, forgetting for a moment who he was talking to. Briefly, Arthur saw the aura of greatness slip from Trotsky, and he became a small boy in the playground, caught red handed at some mischief.

'That?' he said, rubbing his ear. He grinned sheepishly. 'I was . . . holding my pistol . . . trying it for size, and the next thing . . . Bang!'

He chuckled.

It occurred to Arthur how easy it would have been for Trotsky to have made up some more impressive story. That a Tsarist assassin had made an attempt on his life. That he had fired back and in so doing had saved the Revolution. But he did not, and Arthur wondered if it were the sign of a foolish man, or a great one, who has the confidence to tell a story against himself.

6.10 p.m. continued

He has good reason to remember that visit to the Smolny, because it was that same day he met Evgenia.

Evgenia Petrovna Shelepina.

By the time she'd fed him some boiled potatoes, he knew he was already falling in love with her, and that was even before he knew who she really was.

Trotsky's secretary.

He'd gone back to interview Trotsky again two days later, and this time it was Trotsky who'd asked to see Arthur.

Back in room sixty-seven, Arthur had expressed surprise that the Bolsheviks appeared to know all about him. Trotsky seemed almost insulted.

'Do you suppose we are fools? Do you not think it is our business to know who everyone is in this . . . game? A fair analogy, don't you think? You like chess, I believe?'

A prickle ran up the back of Arthur's neck, as again he realised how naive he'd been. Of course they'd been watching him. They were probably watching everyone.

Trotsky wasted no time getting down to business, and began to explain the intricacies of the situation he was in.

'I have to save this Revolution,' he said. 'It is that simple. The Revolution will fail if we cannot end the war with Germany; it is bleeding us dry, in men, and resources. There are two options. Either the war ends for everyone, for Britain *and* Russia, or it ends only for Russia, and you keep fighting Germany.'

Arthur watched as Trotsky spoke, quickly and surely, stroking his small cavalier style beard as he did so.

'I can end the war between Germany and Russia by myself, but then Germany will walk all over us. What I need is for Britain to conclude a peace with Germany too.'

'I see,' Arthur said. 'And what has the British government said to you about that?'

'They have said precisely nothing,' Trotsky said, at once less animated. He sighed. 'The British government still believe that I and Comrade Lenin are German agents sent to topple the country and open the door for invasion.'

Arthur raised his eyebrows.

'How do you know that?'

Trotsky turned to the window, standing near his bullet hole. A dreadful tension hung in the air as he gazed down across the snow-covered gardens of the Smolny. Then he turned.

'And now you are wondering why I am telling you this. Why I am making your journalist's job so easy. Yes?'

Arthur nodded.

'As I said, despite numerous attempts to communicate with your government I have heard nothing from them. Only last night I sent another diplomatic note, via official channels. Once again it has been met with total silence. So, what do you suppose your government would do if they read that Russia is about to conclude a separate peace with Germany?'

'They'd probably want to talk to you very quickly indeed. But how are they going to read this?'

'Oh,' said Trotsky, casually, 'they might read it in their morning paper. Maybe they read the *Daily News* . . . '

He said no more, but he didn't have to.

Arthur knew he was going to do as he'd been asked. Or had he been told?

6.35 p.m.

Arthur leaves the post office, having sent not only the letter to Tabitha, but a telegraphed report for the *News* too.

By the time he gets back to the Elite he's hot and feels dirty. There at the door, is the doorman's girl, Kashka.

'Please? When will the war end?'

'Soon,' Arthur mumbles, forcing a smile, and makes his way wearily up to his floor, up to his room. Only then does he realise he didn't set the scrap of paper in the door frame on his way out.

For a minute he hovers, remembering Lockhart's admonishments, then curses quietly. They are driving him crazy, all these people, with their games and deceits. The British, the Russians; the Bolshevik Reds and Tsarist Whites. If there's someone waiting to murder him on the other side of his door, then so be it. At least if someone pointed a gun at him, he'd know which side he was on.

*

He sits down at his desk.

Above it on the wall, hang three pictures. Two water-colours of the Lakes, painted by his mother. The third is an Orthodox Russian icon of Saint Nicholas. He has had these with him throughout his time in Russia, he had them in the Glinka Street flat in Petrograd, but now he looks at them bitterly. Why do people set such great store by talismans like these?

He catches sight of himself in the mirror, and is shocked by the face that stares back at him. In his mind he carries a very different image of himself, not the thin, unshaven face he sees now.

Ten to seven.

There's plenty of time, still. Too much time, if anything, for doubts and fears to chase each other round his head. But there's enough time, at least, to have a bath and a shave.

He puts out some clean clothes on the bed, then gets his things together from the dresser, his greatcoat from the hook, and locking his door once more, makes his way down the hall to the bathroom shared by the floor. He's in luck, it's empty.

He shuts the door behind him, flicking the latch, and turns the tap on the old boiler that slowly sputters a trickle of hot water into the stained bathtub. He sits down on the toilet seat, knowing it will be a while before the bath is anywhere near ready.

He shuts his eyes, and he thinks about Evgenia.

She's been ill. She's getting better slowly, but was ill for days, and Arthur knows what that's like. He's had dysentery more than once during his time here and there is nothing he can do for her. Not right now. Not tonight.

At least he knows her now.

When he first met her, struck by her beauty and the teasing way she talked to him, it didn't occur to him that there might be more to it. He saw her several more times, and once or twice, when he was leaving the Smolny late in the evening, he had walked her to her tram stop. Only after a few days was he cursed with an awful thought. How had he met her? That first day? He'd bumped into her three times in one evening.

When he saw her for the third time, it was almost as if she was expecting him, waiting for him with her dish of potatoes. Of course, his work and her job meant they would see each other, but perhaps there was more to it than that. She was beautiful and tall and young and clever. Why on earth would she take an interest in an English journalist? Unless . . . someone had put her up to it . . . her boss, perhaps, who just happened to be the effective ruler of Bolshevik Russia.

What had Trotsky said?

'Do you not think we make it our business to know everyone in this game?'

For days he felt sick at the thought he'd been set up,

that she was mere bait, set to trap him.

Then, one night, he'd seen her again at the Smolny.

He needed a pass to attend a meeting at the Tauride palace next day, and worried he'd left it too late, he hurried to get one. To his surprise not only was the building still open, but there was Evgenia at her desk in Trotsky's office.

'Don't you ever go home?' he asked.

'I was about to go,' she said. She stood and began tidying papers.

'I've come for a pass for tomorrow.'

She didn't reply, but sat down again and opened a drawer. She scribbled something on a piece of paper and handed it to him, blowing on the wet ink.

'There you are.'

'No games?'

She frowned at him.

'Usually,' Arthur said, 'There are games to play . . .'

'I'm tired,' she said, and walked to the coat stand in the corner of the room. She was tall, but the huge fur coat still dwarfed her. Arthur noticed with a smile that despite the snow outside she was wearing an elegant pair of heels. He also noticed the curve of her leg before it was hidden by the massive fur.

'Artur Kirilovich,' she said, coming back over. She stood very close as she looked up into his eyes. 'Would you walk me to the tram stop?'

Not wanting to be taken for a fool, Arthur hesitated.

'There's been a lot of trouble on the streets today.

Just for once I don't want to have to watch my back as I go home. Please?'

Her eyes pleaded, and Arthur could not refuse their appeal.

'Of course,' he said. 'Which stop?'

'Thank you,' she said, but she didn't smile. 'It's not far. I live on Vasilievsky. Do you know it?'

'A little,' he said, and they set off down the corridors of the Smolny.

'Do you live alone?' she asked.

'Yes. Do you?'

'My sister . . . '

'Oh yes.'

It was a terrible conversation, and Arthur was glad when they got outside into the swirling cold wind, where it was almost impossible to talk for long anyway.

They walked towards Nevsky Prospect from where Evgenia could catch her tram, and then huddled in a doorway while they waited for it to come. The streets seemed quiet, but she was right, there'd been a lot of scuffles and isolated shootings.

Now they weren't walking, Arthur felt the silence. Someone had to say something.

'How did you . . . ?'

'What?'

'I mean, how did you get into this? The Revolution? To be Trotsky's secretary?'

She shrugged, a gesture almost obliterated by the size of her fur.

114

'I was in the right place at the right time, I suppose.'

'The *right* place?'

She laughed.

'Yes, the right place. My father was a gardener. For the Tsar. My parents live out at Gatchina, it was a Tsarist estate. My sister and I came to the city to work. I worked in the government under the Tsar, and then under Kerensky in the provisional government, and now for Lev Davidovich.'

It was an extraordinary story, but put so simply. Almost everyone and everything else had been swept aside with each change of rule, and yet here was one young girl swimming along with the current behind her. Arthur felt a sudden sorrow for her, and put a gloved hand on her sleeve.

She looked at the hand, then shrieked.

'My tram!'

Without either of them seeing it, the tram had slid up in the wind-blown street. It began to move off, and Evgenia jumped for the running board.

'Thanks so much,' she called, but the words slipped from her mouth, as her foot slipped from the icy step.

Within a moment she was hanging from the step, the heel of one of those expensive shoes caught in the grate, her body dragging along inches from the tram's rear wheels.

Arthur ran.

In his mind he saw the heel snap and the tram run

right over her, and then his mind stopped seeing anymore.

Somehow keeping his footing, he reached her hand and pulled, felt her other hand grab his coat.

Something slipped, and then all he knew was the noise of the tram dying away. They lay in the snow for long seconds, and only then did it all become clear.

'My God,' Arthur said. He rolled over and looked at Evgenia, who sat up. She had a frown on her face like a sulky schoolgirl, and he almost laughed. Almost.

'You could have been . . . '

It didn't need saying.

She stood in front of Arthur, slightly lopsided with one heel missing.

'Those,' she said, 'were expensive shoes.'

Now Arthur did laugh, but offered to find a drozhka to take her home.

'You can't do that,' she protested. 'It's far too expensive. I'll wait for another tram.'

'I'll get a cab and I'll come with you to Vasilievsky. Then I'll get it to take me home. Haven't you had enough of trams for one night?'

'I have had enough of trams,' she said, smiling, and he took that for a yes. He went to find a cab, and as he did, he heard her say something else, though it wasn't clear.

It might have been, 'but not enough of you.' The words were lost in the evening wind.

The accident had changed things, Arthur knew that.

It had brought them closer, helped Arthur to see the real woman, the honesty in her eyes. If Trotsky had set them up, he didn't care. He'd done him a favour.

7.20 p.m.

The bath is a third full with the spitting hot water and now Arthur dares to let the icy cold in to mix with it. He strips absent-mindedly, stirring the water with one foot, then lowers himself gingerly in as hot as he can bear it. Within seconds his skin is pink from the heat, and he feels the pain in his shoulders ease slightly.

His body relaxes, but there is no release for his mind. His soul is tired. The wave that has rolled through Russia has been easy to ride. He's been swept along, but nonetheless there's horror waiting just beneath the water, and every now and again, one of the horrors surfaces.

Almost right from the start, it was unclear whose side he was on.

He was summoned to the Smolny one day early in January not to see Trotsky or Lenin, but another of the Bolshevik clan. Karl Radek possibly outshone his more powerful colleagues in terms of intellect, and certainly eccentricity. Arthur was shown into an office where he was greeted by a tiny man, with pointed nose and clean-shaven chin, wild and wiry hair, small round glasses, and a pipe seemingly glued to the corner of his mouth. He reminded Arthur not so much of a man as a pixie, or some sort of hobgoblin.

On the table beside him lay a collection of books, and some other items too. Arthur immediately recognised them as his own. When he left Stockholm, he'd feared a difficult journey and had asked Vorovsky to send much of his stuff after him. Vorovsky had sent them, just not to the right person.

'You had no business to open that!' Arthur declared.

'Mr Ransome,' he said, smiling, 'it's a pleasure to meet you.'

Thrown off guard, Arthur returned the handshake.

'What I said to myself,' Radek went on, 'is what kind of man owns such diverse and wonderful things! These books alone. What have we here?'

He began to rummage, like a squirrel foraging, all the time a generous smile on his face.

'Ah ha! Shakespeare! So I know the man is a good Englishman. "To be or not to be", yes? "Whether 'tis nobler in the mind to suffer the slings and arrows of . . ."'

He broke off.

'But why am I reciting Shakespeare to you? You are the Englishman!'

He laughed.

'I am a Pole,' he said. 'I'm a Pole who speaks Polish badly because I talked too much German when I was in exile with Mr Lenin and the others. But when I speak Russian I sound Polish, do I not? I speak French too, but abominably. Hmm. But we were talking about you. How rude of me. Here we have a chess set, with folding board and miniature pieces. Clever. So we know the owner has a keen and shrewd mind.'

Arthur was pleased to see it again, but didn't assume his things would be returned.

'And here we have some more books. One on chess. Interesting. Does this mean that our man is modest; willing to admit that there might always be something new to learn? That he doesn't know it all. I think perhaps this is true? And what about these books? One on fishing. So what. So a man who can fish might be able to provide for himself when those around him are starving. And a book on navigation. Navigation. You are learning the rudiments of how to travel across the sea unaided. Does this perhaps tell me that the man is engaged in certain hidden activities? That he is a spy?'

'No,' Arthur protested.

Radek laughed again.

'No,' he said. 'No. I know you are not yet a spy.'

There it was again. Language is a subtle but vicious killer. What did he mean by 'yet'?

'Would you like to take your things away or shall we have someone bring them to your apartment?'

'You mean I can have them back?'

'Certainly. What would I want with a book on fishing? And Shakespeare, I know my Shakespeare well enough, I think.'

Arthur hesitated, looking at the contents of the parcel strewn across the table.

'Would you mind sending it on?'

'Of course. And now Mr Ransome, can I offer you some tea?'

He accepted, and soon the parcel was forgotten. As they spoke Arthur saw why he had opened it; there was no great sinister meaning behind it, but simply that Radek was a small boy in a big world, curious and inquisitive. Arthur stayed far longer than he realised, and fell into a long conversation about everything from chess to revolution, but it was another small warning, Arthur knew. Nothing he did, nothing he said, nothing he owned, would be his alone.

He started working for Buchanan, the British Ambassador. He'd been asked to find out what he could about Trotsky, and he did, reporting back in good faith. And if he learned anything interesting from Evgenia about her employers, well, that simply showed that he understood the game.

But if Arthur started to understand what he was doing, others did not.

He was in Buchanan's office, a few days before the kind old Ambassador left Russia for good. A week later and Lockhart arrived, and then things changed entirely, but that day, Arthur was reporting to Buchanan, as usual.

Just then the door flew open, and an officer burst in. He pointed at Arthur.

'You sir,' he declared, his nostrils quivering, 'should be shot!'

Arthur had never met him before but knew him by sight. General Knox was the British Military Attaché to Petrograd.

Buchanan raised a hand to try to stop Knox, but he was in no mood to stop.

'Sir George, I've been watching this man, and his . . . activities. He is a Red! He has been consorting with the Bolsheviks, and should be considered a traitor. He ought to be dealt with as such!'

Arthur tried to protest his innocence, but Knox ignored him completely apart from occasionally waving a finger in his direction. Buchanan, meanwhile, already weakened by his illness, was in no condition for a fight, and simply waited for the storm to pass.

Knox ended his tirade and looked expectantly at Buchanan, like a dog waiting for a bone. Arthur would have found him comical, but he knew that he was the bone Knox wanted.

Buchanan lifted his gaze from his desk to Knox.

'General,' he said, 'Mr Ransome is an agent of the British Embassy, and therefore the British government.

Please be good enough to treat him accordingly. You may go.'

It was over. Knox stood rooted to the spot briefly and then, as the colour rose in his cheeks, spun on his heel and slammed the door behind him.

Buchanan forced a weak smile on Arthur.

'Talk to Trotsky, find out what he really wants. Do your job. Then come and tell me.'

Arthur nodded, and did as he was told, but it all came to nothing.

Next day, Buchanan left for England, and a week later, Lockhart arrived to act in his place.

7.55 p.m.

The cold tap drips in the bath, almost hypnotising Arthur. He stirs himself and stretches his long legs, resting his feet on the wall above the taps. His thoughts drift some more and a face comes to mind.

Lockhart.

When Arthur learned he'd returned to Russia, he was surprised, to put it mildly. Lockhart had been sent home from his position in Moscow in disgrace. There'd been an affair with a Russian Jewess; she was married, and then again, so was he. The official story was ill-health, returning home to rest, honourable leave of absence. The usual humbug, but Arthur knew the truth, had had the gossip from the Embassy corridors, that Lockhart had been a bad boy. It wasn't even so much that he'd had an affair, it was that he hadn't been able to keep it a secret.

For a man in his profession, that was a crime in itself.

It was unforgivable.

And yet, he had been forgiven, because he came back to Petrograd in January.

The Embassy was always a good standby for a decent plate of food; that was something Arthur had learned. As things got harder through that winter, he found his visits coincided more and more often with lunch.

On the prowl one day for food and news, in that order, he got more than he expected.

Lockhart.

Arthur's heart rose the moment he saw him. He rushed over, shaking the Scot warmly by the hand.

'Steady on, Ransome,' he said, laughing.

'It's so good to see a friendly face,' Arthur said. 'Everyone else has left.'

'And I bet you thought you'd seen the last of me, eh?'

Arthur shrugged.

'Nothing surprises me anymore. After the Ambassador left I didn't know who would replace him.'

'Oh, I'm not replacing him, he was an Ambassador, whereas I . . . ' he paused. 'If I'm replacing anyone, I'm replacing you.'

He smiled.

'Don't worry, I've no interest in journalism. I've been sent here as head of a special mission. To make and keep contact with Trotsky and the Bolsheviks. Something that seems to have been your sole responsibility up till now.'

'I see. Sir George didn't mention you were coming.'

'Would it have been any of your business? Anyway, he may not have known. I was only told myself just before Christmas.'

'You knew he was ill.'

'Yes,' Lockhart nodded. 'Saw him in Norway on my way out here. The cruiser that sent me here was to collect him and take him home. He seemed pretty badly off, but you know, you could see he was relieved to be out of Russia.'

'It does that to some people.'

'Listen, Ransome, it's lunchtime, fancy a bite to eat?'

Arthur smiled to himself, delighted his little scheme had worked again.

'I have to admit,' he said, 'The food here . . . '

'No,' Lockhart said, quietly. 'Not here. Let's go out. Yes?'

They walked through the city's ice-bound streets, trying and failing to find a restaurant that was both open and with the appearance of somewhere they might actually want to eat. Arthur mildly cursed himself for the presumption that he was going to get his teeth into Embassy food again. Eventually, they stumbled across a place. A vegetarian restaurant, called 'I Eat Nobody', it was the wit of the name as much as anything else that took them inside.

'Probably the safest place to eat anyway,' Arthur said as they sat down. 'There are some bad stories circulating about the little meat that is available. Species-wise.'

'Species-wise?' Lockhart grimaced.

Arthur nodded.

'Species-wise.'

Over bowls of steaming borsch Lockhart told Arthur about his mission.

'The government still isn't prepared to recognise the Bolsheviks officially. The attitude is still one of calculated indifference. The policy is that there is no policy. But, there are those, and Mr Lloyd George is among them, who have read the newspaper reports of certain journalists,' he looked straight into Arthur's eyes, 'and feel that there should be some kind of relationship with the Bolsheviks.'

He took a mouthful of the beetroot soup while Arthur pondered the fact that the Prime Minister of Great Britain had actually been influenced by something he'd written.

'I'm here to head up a mission of official contact with Messrs. Trotsky and Lenin. Unofficially, of course.'

Arthur smiled.

'Naturally. Which rather makes me redundant as a go-between.'

'Officially yes. But unofficially, I . . . '

He stopped, and put his spoon down.

'Arthur, you have to tell me something, and you have to tell me straight. Are you a Bolshevik?'

Arthur's laugh made the few other people in the near-empty restaurant look sharply round.

'Ransome,' Lockhart said. 'An answer, if you please.'

'Sorry,' he said. 'Sorry. No. No, of course, I'm not a Bolshevik. I'm a journalist. It's my job to talk to them. By that logic . . . '

'Fair enough. I believe you, but this is a strange world we are living in, and not everyone is what they seem. Half the world still believes Trotsky is a German agent sent to topple Russia from the inside.'

'That's nonsense.'

'I know it's nonsense, but that's not the point. It's what people believe is true that matters, not what actually is true.'

There was something else Lockhart was driving at, but Arthur let it pass, and let him talk.

'You need to be careful, Arthur. And I need your help, so you've got to stay out of trouble.'

'My help?'

'I may now be the official channel from Britain to the Bolsheviks, but you know them in a way I don't. You can get me into places, get interviews, contacts.'

'That's fine. I can do that.'

'Yes, you can, but only if you're not locked in a prison cell.'

He picked up his spoon again and began to work on the soup once more.

'That sounds like a threat.'

'It might be, but it's not from me. However, there are those who think you are not to be trusted, Arthur. There are even some who think you are an agent.'

'An agent?' Arthur said, doubtfully.

'Dammit, Arthur,' Lockhart whispered across the table fiercely. 'A spy! Do you understand me? A Russian spy.'

Arthur nodded gently, and there was no laughter on his lips this time.

'Who are these people?' he asked.

'Some ministers. The head of Scotland Yard. People at the Foreign Office, the Secret Service. Oh, and some of the Americans.'

'Americans?' Arthur spluttered.

'Keep your voice down,' said Lockhart. 'Yes, Americans. Listen, I told you that this is a strange world. You may be what you seem, but not everyone else is. You know Sissons?'

'Head of the American Mission?'

'Head of the American Mission, and a spy to boot. He has formed the opinion that you are also an agent; the only difference is that he can't make up his mind whether you're a British one or a Russian one.'

Arthur shook his head in disbelief. He had little time for Sissons, but nonetheless had spoken to him frequently over the last few days. With a dead weight in his stomach he remembered that they'd even arranged to meet the following day to get passes for the Constituent Assembly. He began replaying all his conversations with him, trying to recall what he'd said and what it could mean.

'I'd stop that if I were you,' Lockhart said, having guessed what he was doing. 'You'll go mad that way. Just be careful from now on. Because I need you.'

8.10 p.m.

Arthur lies in the bath.

He has propped his pocket watch on the side of the sink, but can't make out the time as the face has steamed up. For a moment he panics, then forces himself to relax. He can't have been in the bathroom for more than an hour at the very most; that still gives him nearly two hours to get dressed and go to meet Lockhart.

He waits for his heart to stop thumping.

The meeting point is fifteen minutes away, at a stroll; a small seedy bar called Finland. And then on to wherever Lockhart has set up his denouement. For that's how it feels to Arthur, it feels like a finale, an end game.

The analogy with chess springs to his mind again. It was Radek who made the comparison first, wasn't it? Or Trotsky? It doesn't matter now, whichever of them said it, it's true. Arthur loves a good chess puzzle, he's played games at the strangest times, and found it clears his head and calms his mind. Once, years ago, when he was away

131

at the front near Tarnopol, he played chess with a young officer even as shells fell in the distance. They'd played one game which Arthur had won by a lucky stroke, then the officer had had to mount up and ride away.

'I'll give you a rematch when I get back,' he'd called, but Arthur never saw him again.

Arthur sits up in the bath and props his shaving mirror behind the cold tap. He soaps his chin. If I am in a chess game, he thinks, I know which piece I am.

A pawn.

Bizarrely, though, he's still not sure which side he belongs to. He's a pawn in no man's land, caught between the white British knights and the red Russian rooks. But each side thinks they own him, and that scares him. He thinks of the move in chess called the pawn sacrifice. A pawn is of little worth, and can easily be expended if there is a chance of a greater reward to be had.

No, he tells himself.

No, he's on the British side. He's agreed to Lockhart's scheme, for good or for bad, and it's too late to start dithering about it now.

8.20 p.m.

Arthur gets out of the bath carefully, feeling at least a hundred. As he stands he sees his body in miniature in the shaving mirror. God! He's so thin. Even the relative comfort of the Elite is not providing him enough to keep him well fed.

Too bad, he thinks. There are people worse off, all across Moscow, across Russia. There are stories coming in from the unknown depths of Samara province that people have resorted to the ultimate taboo, and are eating meat of a very familiar nature. Not everyone believes the stories of cannibals, but there are those who do. Even in the bleakest winter days back in Petrograd such an idea would have been unthinkable.

Arthur wraps a towel round his waist, drapes his greatcoat across his shoulders and makes his way back down the corridor to his room, now completely oblivious of scraps of paper, door frames, and even unseen gunmen.

Closing the door behind him, he slips the coat back

onto its hook, and checks he has put out all the clothes he will wear, as if preparing for some magical ritual.

It was only a couple of months after Lockhart returned to Russia that they moved to Moscow.

'You and I have been speaking the same language,' Lockhart said to Arthur, as they had a drink in the bar of the Astoria. 'You and I. We both think that the best thing that our government could do, for Russia and for the war, is to help the Bolsheviks. Yes?'

'Are we alone in that view?' Arthur asked.

'Things are changing,' he said. 'Good God, things are changing all the time. Our government, Arthur, is trying to make up its mind whether to ignore the Bolsheviks, or invade Russia and restore the Tsar and the rest of White Russia.'

'Invade? But that would be . . . .'

Lockhart ignored the pointless remark. He sat opposite Arthur, their knees almost touching, but staring at his hands as he spoke.

'Red or white, white or red. Who knows which colour pieces they'll choose . . . ? And everything is changing, every day. Everyone is leaving.'

'Everyone?' Arthur asked. Lockhart glanced up at his friend, seemed to shake himself, and got back to business.

'The Bolsheviks are leaving Petrograd. The new German front line is a short train ride from here; the

Reds are moving their capital to Moscow, as of old. Napoleon never managed to capture it. I think they figure that since Napoleon failed, the Kaiser will too. But it was the winter that stopped Napoleon, and spring is almost here. Anyway, they're going to up and run to Moscow, and everyone else is simply running away. The French, the Chinese, the Japanese Ambassadors are leaving.'

Everyone. The Bolsheviks had decided that Petrograd was too close to the German army, who were advancing in fits and starts towards the city. When the Bolsheviks went, so did everyone else; all the foreign embassies, the Japanese, the Germans, the French, the British; and so did anyone else with any interest in them. Lockhart and his mission. The few remaining journalists. Arthur. There was nothing left for him in Petrograd. He shut his flat up, having given his landlady an exorbitant sum of roubles to keep it on for him, just in case. He was happy enough to be fleeced by her, it was only money, and there were more important things than money.

Evgenia had gone too, following Trotsky to Moscow with the other Bolsheviks. He hadn't even seen her before she went; he'd been sent on some wild goose chase by Lockhart. In the event of a German invasion of Russia, and the British having to leave Moscow, they needed a bolthole halfway to the northern coast. Lockhart had asked Arthur to go to a godforsaken town called Vologda, and to 'claim' a building there suitable for use as the British Embassy if need be.

'Claim it?' Arthur had asked.

'Stick a flag on it, man!' Lockhart said.

'And where do I get a flag from?'

'Use your ingenuity. And get a move on.'

'I only earn a journalist's wages, you know.'

'All your expenses will be covered,' Lockhart assured him, 'by the British government.'

Arthur did as he was told.

In the end, he had borrowed a flag from the one of the British cruisers imprisoned by the frozen waters of the Neva, and had made the fruitless journey to Vologda. He had learned one thing from the trip, though, one very important thing. While there, muddled news from the peace talks with Germany led Moscow to think that a German invasion was imminent. Lenin of all people had telegraphed to Arthur and his travelling companions to let them know the news, so they might take whatever action they saw fit. For the foreigners, this meant running for home. Arthur read the telegram with disbelief, not at what Lenin had to say, but at an extra message tacked on the end, addressed purely to him.

It was from Evgenia.

'As this means war,' she said, 'you will no doubt have to travel again. But you have my best wishes for a happy journey.'

Why on earth would Trotsky's secretary have the impertinence to adulterate Lenin's telegram with a

136

message to an English journalist? Unless that Englishman meant something to her?

He found her again, his very first day in Moscow.

Lockhart got him a room at the Elite, but Arthur discovered that all the Bolshevik party were staying at the National Hotel. The plan was to move into the Kremlin, but with their sudden arrival from Petrograd, it wasn't yet ready.

Arthur found the Bolsheviks in disarray at the National, and was treated to the sight of Lenin sitting on a pile of packing cases in the lobby. Lenin called him over.

'Comrade Ransome! What are you British doing now?'

Arthur feigned ignorance, but he knew what Lenin was talking about. Lockhart had told him unbelievable news. An admiral and a company of British marines had landed at Murmansk and captured the town. Lockhart didn't seem to know their further intentions, but it was hard to see it as anything other than an expeditionary invasion force.

Lenin wasn't fooled.

'Your government refuses to talk to us, and the moment we seem to sign a peace with Germany, you invade our country!'

'I'm sure the British government is only seeking to help Russians.'

'Maybe so, Comrade Ransome. But which Russians? Red? Or White?'

Arthur shifted uncomfortably, and as his gaze shifted, his eyes fell on the person he'd really come to find. He made a few limp excuses and as casually as he could, walked over to Evgenia, his head full of nothing to say.

She turned.

'You came back!'

Arthur smiled, then laughed. It felt difficult at first. Then wonderful.

'Of course I did,' he said. 'It was the only way to make a happy journey.'

Evgenia looked puzzled.

'You wished me a happy journey. One that comes back to you.'

He paused, trying to ignore the people milling around them.

'I had to come back. To see you. To be with you.'

Evgenia blushed, showing Arthur a vulnerable side he'd not seen before. Fighting the urge to put his arms around her and kiss her, he put a hand lightly on her sleeve. Already he could see Lenin looking in their direction, and a warning bell rang in his head.

'Listen,' he whispered. 'Lockhart's throwing a party at the Elite. Tomorrow night. Say you'll come?'

She smiled, and before he could react took a quick step towards him and brushed his lips with hers.

She nodded, and hurried away.

138

This is what you want.

Arthur stood alone in the busy hallway, trying to blot everything from his mind but the feel of her lips on his, before the memory slipped away for good.

8.50 p.m.

Arthur dresses, slowly.

Was this how a knight would have felt, before going into battle? Each piece of clothing he puts on feels like a piece of armour. His trousers are cuisses, his socks are greaves. His shirt is a cuirass, the collar a ventail. His boots are sabatons, his jacket a surcoat. But if he thinks he is armouring himself, it is an illusion; a bullet will sail clean through his armour and his skin to burn the flesh beneath.

Nevertheless, it helps. It's just another talisman, but he's taking all he can get.

He knows he is no knight, though at least, like the hero in a fairy tale or romance, he finally knows what his quest is. His purpose.

He checks his watch, for the twentieth time.

Not long.

He runs over the plan once more, or as much as he knows of it. He wonders if Lockhart has held anything

140

back. Maybe he doesn't trust him entirely.

They'll meet at ten, at the Finland bar. Then Lockhart will tell Arthur where to go and meet the two Latvians, and where to take them.

Simple.

So simple.

Arthur ties his tie. It's the only one he has now; the rest are all in the flat in Petrograd. As he ties it memories return of the last time he wore it; Lockhart's party downstairs in the hotel dining room. He turns and looks at the bed, and smiles.

He got there early.

The first guests were arriving at the dining room of the Elite, which had been turned into an impromptu cabaret. Tables were being moved into place, a few early diners being seated, and Lockhart surveyed everything. The hotel knew what it was doing, but tonight it was only doing so with Lockhart's money.

Arthur saw Lockhart and headed for him, something on his mind.

'I thought Robins was Head of the Red Cross.'

'He is,' Lockhart said, waving at someone across the room. 'Look, do we have to talk business tonight, Arthur?'

'Yes, we do. I'll leave you alone, just answer me some questions. We were out walking this afternoon and we were stopped by some Red Guards. Routine check. I opened my coat like a good boy. Robins legged it and escaped over a wall.'

Arthur hesitated, staring hard at Lockhart.

'He's a spy, isn't he?'

Lockhart whipped round and glared at him, though no one was in earshot.

'Just how stupid are you going to be?' he snapped.

'As stupid as I have to be. Is he a spy?'

'He's Head of the American Red Cross mission . . .'

'And he's a spy, too, isn't he?'

'Does this matter, Arthur? Why do you need to know? Are you going to print it in your newspaper?'

'Of course not. I'm not *that* stupid.'

'Good, because stupid people end up dead people. No, I am not being dramatic, Arthur. That's how it is. And you'd be wise to keep your nose out of it.'

'Apart from when you need my help,' Arthur said. 'And then you're only too keen for me to get my nose dirty.'

Lockhart sighed and held up his hand.

'Guilty,' he said quietly. 'You're right. I simply want you to understand what's going on here.'

'I thought that was *my* point,' Arthur said. 'I want to know what's going on. I want to know who everyone is. What they are. I need to know who I can trust.'

Lockhart sipped from his glass.

'And you,' Arthur said, 'You're a spy too, aren't you?'

Lockhart put down the glass and eyed Arthur.

'That's a dangerous thing to say, Arthur,' he said eventually. 'Very dangerous. I suggest you be very careful about who you say things like that to. Luckily for you,

you can trust me. Remember that.'

Lockhart stood up, but one thing was obvious; he hadn't denied it.

'Look,' he said, 'there's your girlfriend. I'll leave you to it. To her.'

Arthur turned to see Evgenia, who smiled and walked over.

'Listen,' Lockhart whispered before she made it to the table. 'Try and have some fun tonight, for God's sake.'

8.50 p.m. continued

The cabaret was extraordinary.

There was food. Lots of food. So much food that it seemed impossible that they could be in the same country where horse was more or less the only meat available day to day. Course after course was placed in front of them, all carried high and proud on the shoulders of a stream of white-aproned, black-tied waiters.

Hors d'oeuvres that defied imagination. Snails in mushrooms, blinis with caviar, red and black, smoked salmon. Raw venison that looked like beetroot but was chewy like rubber, scallops in their shells, and moose from Finland.

Arthur ate slowly and steadily, but after a while, the drink took over. At every conceivable moment Arthur found a charochka forced into his hands; a glass of champagne intended to be drunk in a single draught. Laughter followed, and then more champagne, and all this a mere sideshow to the epic consumption of vodka.

Evgenia and Arthur sat alone.

'What would Trotsky say if he knew you were here?'

he asked her, and she pulled a face.

'I don't want to think about him tonight, Arthur.'

'All right,' Arthur said, and then, to his own horror, found himself asking her to dance. Lockhart's weakness for gypsy music had materialised, and he'd paid for musicians and dancers to perform all evening. Infectious gypsy music filled the air like the perfume of evening flowers, irresistibly sweet.

'I'd love to,' Evgenia said.

She pulled him over to where a small dancefloor had been cleared among the tables and chairs, and they whirled around for a while to a frantic tune on the violin. Lockhart stood at the edge of the dancefloor clapping time with his hands and stamping his feet. A pretty girl with dark waves of hair clung to his arm, smiling as Evgenia and Arthur came to a crashing halt at the end of the song.

The band seemed to take pity on them, and their next song was a slow and mournful tune, in waltz time. Here was something Arthur was more familiar with, and they stepped slowly around each other and the room, his hands holding her hand and hip, his legs pushing hers to guide their way through the other dancers.

As if seeing her for the first time, he smiled at Evgenia, and she smiled back, her beautiful eyes twinkled in the golden candlelight, and the music wound its way through his heart and there and then, made him love her.

'What is it?' she whispered. 'You look so serious.'

'I am serious,' Arthur said.

'And you look a little drunk.'

'I might be that too,' he said, and laughed.

The world might be ripping itself to pieces in a war too dreadful to know, but for one evening, he forgot everything but Evgenia. He wanted her in a way he'd never wanted any woman before. He wanted to make her happy.

It was late, and the room had emptied somewhat as even a few of the Russians found the pace too hard and crawled home. The whole scene must have been played out a thousand nights or more in the past, but the war and the Revolution had changed that. Here, for one night only, was a reminder of the hedonism of former days, and the only sign that said otherwise was the sight of the kitchen staff standing in the doorways, watching and smiling and clapping along to the music. Maids stood, scarves round their heads, dressed to go home but unable to tear themselves away from the happiness.

Lockhart was by now the willing victim of the gypsies who brought countless charochki for to him to drink, which he did happily, and then requested the same song, again and again. It was a bittersweet love song, so deep and full of yearning that only Russia could have created it. As Lockhart listened his eyes drifted far away and took him to another place, another time.

At the end of the song, the girl on his arm planted a huge kiss on his mouth, and the singer, a small man with a giant voice leant over to him.

'The gentleman is almost drunk!' he whispered so loud the whole room heard, and the whole room laughed.

Lockhart stood up, waving a hand in the air to get everyone's attention.

'Almost,' he said, falling backwards over a table like a horse trying to ice-skate. The girl he was with made a noise that was a laugh and a shriek combined and ran round the table to look for him, a jug of water in her hand.

Arthur turned to say something to Evgenia, who put her finger up to his lips, then pulled it away again, and kissed him.

Arthur smiled.

'Do you realise,' he said, 'that you have the most beautiful face?'

She leaned in towards him.

Arthur held her for a long time, and later held her upstairs in his room, and in his bed, until finally they found sleep.

When he woke he was alone. Evgenia had gone, leaving Arthur with memories and a headache.

9.20 p.m.

Arthur snaps from his reverie of Lockhart's party that night, downstairs, such a short way from where he stands now, watching dusk fall over Moscow.

'Everything's changing,' Lockhart had said.

He was right. Everything had changed, including him.

For months, Lockhart was the only one who shared Arthur's opinion, that England should help Russia, not invade it. But that too had changed.

'It's over, Arthur,' Lockhart said. 'It's over. If the Bolsheviks give in to Germany, then Germany will invade Russia, and we'll probably lose the war. With Russia out of their hair, the Germans will overrun us in France. The only hope now is to put the Tsarists back on the throne.'

Arthur couldn't believe what he was hearing.

'You can't mean that.'

'I do. What's more I've been doing something about it.'

He pulled a pocket book from inside his jacket.

'We've been raising funds,' he said, 'from White

148

Russians. I'm only the banker, but the money's been passed on to counter-revolutionaries.'

Arthur shook his head, putting his hands out as if trying to push Lockhart away.

'Don't tell me,' he said. 'I don't want to know . . . '

'Dammit, Arthur!' Lockhart shouted. 'You have to know. You have to understand. I work for the British government. I do their bidding. That's all there is to it. If I'm told to collect money from rich exiled Russians and pass it to White soldiers, then that's what I'll do.'

He stopped and Arthur breathed deeply.

'And the book?'

'A record of the transactions. Don't worry, it's all encrypted. Still, if anything ever happens to me I want you to destroy it. All right?'

Arthur nodded.

'Nothing's going to happen to you, Robert.'

Lockhart smiled.

'How can you be so sure?'

'You have life written all over you. Some people bear tragedy on their faces; loss, death, whatever it might be. But you have life.'

'Is this some kind of poetic writer's thing?'

'Come on,' Arthur said, 'You're not only the pragmatist you make yourself out to be. You feel things too.'

Lockhart nodded.

'So which are you, then Arthur? What's written on your face? Life? Or tragedy?'

Arthur's smile faded.

'I don't know,' he said. 'It's not something you can see in yourself.'

He stood up and stretched his legs, turned to leave.

'Arthur,' Lockhart said, abruptly. 'There's something I need you to do . . .'

9.20 p.m. continued

But Arthur hadn't agreed.

Not at first.

How could he do anything against the Bolsheviks when he was in love with one of them?

Then again, who was she, exactly, this gardener's daughter from Gatchina? Was even that true?

She came to his room. It was early spring then, still cold, but sunny.

When Arthur opened the door and saw Evgenia in her long black winter fur, he tried to pull her inside, but she resisted.

'No,' she said, 'I can't.'

'Then why did you come? Don't you want to see me?'

'Yes, but not here. Not now. Tomorrow? We could go out of the city . . . then we can talk. Meet me downstairs tomorrow at nine, yes? Oh, I brought you a present.'

She handed him a small parcel.

Silently he opened it and found inside a small but

exquisite silver samovar.

Arthur was shocked.

'This must have cost a fortune . . . how did you . . . ?'

'Shh. I didn't pay for it,' Evgenia said quickly. 'It's from the old days. Somehow it ended up in our office and *they* didn't pay for it either. When I saw it I thought of you, and knew you had to have it. Look.'

She showed him the side of the metal teapot where, in English letters, were his own initials, AR.

'That's very strange,' Arthur said. 'I wonder who it belonged to.'

'You're welcome,' said Evgenia, slyly.

'Sorry, yes, thank you. It's wonderful. I'll make you tea with it from now on.'

'But not today. I must go.'

She went, and Arthur spent the day in an agony of waiting. He slept badly that night and was awake by seven. He took breakfast and then killed an hour by trying to write letters to his mother and to Geoff, though each one he hated more than the last, and they all ended up in the wastepaper basket.

At last it was nine, and Arthur waited on the pavement outside the Elite.

A horse and cab pulled up. Evgenia sat waiting inside.

'Do you have money?' she asked Arthur as he climbed aboard.

'Yes. Enough,' he said, and they sped away through the streets.

It didn't take long to reach the outskirts and then the country opened out under the rolling wheels of the cab. It seemed to Arthur that he hadn't seen grass or trees or even the sky for years, and yet here they all were, bright and bursting with life. Arthur kept one eye on Evgenia all the time, who seemed to relax visibly as the city disappeared over the horizon.

They spoke about the Revolution, and her family. They spoke about how she'd ended up working for the Bolsheviks.

'Trotsky likes me,' she said. 'He knows I work hard, that he can trust me. Those things are hard to find these days.'

Then they talked, finally, as the cab turned back to the city, about the one thing that had gone unspoken since the night at the party.

'Is something wrong?' Arthur said.

'No, it's just that . . . it's not easy.'

'You mean, you and me?'

Evgenia nodded.

'Why? Because I'm English? Because I'm still married? Divorces take a long time in England . . . '

'No,' Evgenia said. 'No. It's nothing like that.'

'Then what?'

'What do you think? One day you may leave Russia. You may be forced to go, you may decide to leave. And then, who knows? And in the meantime . . . let me put it this way. Who do I work for?'

'Trotsky. The Bolsheviks.'

'Yes, and do you think they don't know about you and me? Well, they do. And if you think that's all there is to it you can think again.'

'They're not happy about it?'

She laughed, a short and joyless laugh.

'Far from it. They're rather pleased that one of their people has such close contact with an Englishman. An Englishman with such connections as you have. To Lockhart, to the Ambassador, to the Americans. A man who knows what's going on in the Allies' camp.'

'They want you to use me? To spy on me?'

'They want me to tell them everything you tell me. Very simple.'

She fell silent, and Arthur with her. The cab rolled on back towards the city, now following the river. Already they could see the walls and spires of the Kremlin in the distance, where people with cold hearts made even colder propositions.

'This is a war,' Evgenia said at last, 'that's the way people are in a war. So we are used, Arthur, you and me. Two small people who want to love each other, but we are to be used.'

All too soon, they were back at the Elite. Rooks cawed and scudded through the air above their heads as the horse clattered to a stop.

Arthur thought about what Evgenia had said, as he stepped down and held out a hand to help her down.

'Listen to me,' he said. 'I won't let this stop us. They want you to tell them everything I tell you. That's only a problem if I tell you anything that puts us in trouble, you and me, or our friends, Russian or English. And I won't. In the meantime you can keep your end of the bargain and tell them what a helpful and friendly Englishman I am, willing to consort freely with Bolsheviks of all shapes and sizes.'

Then, as she stood on the step of the cab, he kissed her tenderly, both heedless of who might be watching.

She walked away along the street, and Arthur made his own way back up to his room. He was desperate to feel nothing but happiness, but too many doubts nagged away at him. Suppose she was playing this game better than he imagined? Maybe he'd played right into their hands, letting himself be ruled by his heart. His head told him there would be trouble ahead, and not just in Russia. It would be no simple thing to love this Russian girl.

He thought of Ivy, and immediately of Tabitha. He thought of his mother and Geoff, but right at that moment, England, and everyone in it, seemed so very far away.

9.20 p.m. continued

Life in Moscow was getting more and more precarious. Bands of rogue anarchists roamed the city, pillaging for food, and were holed up in numerous palaces in the better areas. They raided the American mission building, stealing a car belonging to Robins, the head of the mission, but the disturbances had not gone unnoticed by the Bolsheviks. Trotsky had decided to act, and set up a special police force he called the Extraordinary Commission, the Cheka.

Lockhart knocked on Arthur's door, early one morning in April.

'Did you hear the shooting last night?'

It would have been impossible to have missed it.

'There were twenty-six raids,' Lockhart said. 'Get your coat.'

'Where are we going?'

'We've been invited to survey the Cheka's handiwork . . .'

'Who by?'

'The Cheka. They want me to see what they've been

up to. They want a western journalist to see it too.'

Outside a motor car stood running. In the back stood an officer, who introduced himself as Peters, second in command of the new special police force.

Soon, they were driving through some of the best streets in Moscow, stopping now and again to survey the result of the Cheka's assault on the anarchist strongholds. House after house was the same, most of them badly smashed up by bullets outside and in. The mess and filth were hideous; the houses had been looted by both the anarchists before the raid and hooligans during the day after it.

Along the Povarskaya, once one of the most fashionable streets in Moscow, half a dozen houses had suffered the same fate.

The car stopped and Peters invited Lockhart and Arthur to follow him.

Arthur turned to Lockhart as they walked up the steps of the nearest house.

'Why are they showing all this? To impress us . . . ?'

'Or to scare us?'

They fell silent as they made their way through the once luxurious house into a large atrium from which vast staircases curved up to the first floor. The destruction was terrible. Broken bottles lay everywhere. Pictures were pocked with bullet holes, or slashed by swords. Excrement mixed with the stains of wine and other fluids on what remained of the Persian carpets.

The dead lay where they had fallen. Among the

bodies were officers and other men in uniform, students, boys of twenty or less, and shaven-headed men who had probably been convicts until the Revolution freed them. They picked a route past the bodies, trying not to gag at the stench. Upstairs, they found an even worse scene; the anarchists had clearly been caught in the middle of an orgy. In a perverted mockery of the party Lockhart threw at the Elite, the scene before them filled Arthur with horror. A massive table lay spread with food and drink of all kinds, glasses and champagne bottles, plates and cutlery, yet now the table was also filled with other, more horrific things.

On the floor lay a young woman, face down.

Peters, the Cheka man, walked over to her and, with his boot, turned her body over. She was no more than twenty. She had been shot through the back of her neck, and a large clump of hair and blood had congealed into a purple mass on her shoulder.

He shrugged his shoulders.

'Prostitutka,' he said, without emotion. 'Perhaps it is for the best.'

Lockhart and Arthur looked at each other. They nodded at Peters as if they'd seen enough and left the building.

Very soon they were back at the Elite and without a word went their separate ways, as if an unspoken agreement not to talk had been made.

Back in his room, Arthur stared across Moscow, towards the Povarskaya.

What had he seen?

What had he *done*? For some reason he'd felt guilty, looking at the dead prostitute, as guilty as if he'd pulled the trigger himself.

As they'd left the building, Peters had told them what a proud achievement this was for the Bolsheviks. Ever since the Revolution the anarchists had been out of control, he said, a thorn in the side, and it had taken decisive Bolshevik action to rid the city of the plague. In time, the Cheka would establish discipline and order throughout revolutionary Russia. A hundred people had been shot in the raids, a further five hundred arrested. The night had been a complete success.

If this was success, Arthur wanted none of it.

He was lost.

He'd been there, at the Revolution, seen the new Russia born, with hopes of democracy for the greatest nation on earth. He'd supported the Bolshevik cause in his articles for the *News*, and had helped Lockhart to try and get London to understand what their hopes for Russia were all about.

The Bolsheviks had put a bullet through those hopes.

For the first time Arthur admitted to himself that he was scared. Not just of the violence that occurred so casually, day in and day out, but scared in a more profound way. He wondered if he had any control in his life, and that maybe, he'd never had any control. Had he ever made a choice in his life that was his, or had he always been part of someone else's devices? His parents, his teachers, bullies at school, friends and lovers. The British, the Russians. He thought for a while and came up with an answer; one choice that *was* truly his. He'd left Ivy and come to Russia. With that decision, he'd left Tabitha, too.

He turned from the window, but the picture in his mind would not shift.

Standing by the prostitute's body, Lockhart and Arthur had seen the look in each other's eyes. What should they have done, when Peters rolled the girl over onto her broken back? Should they have screamed at him, railed and fought with him, denounced him and his Cheka and the Bolsheviks too?

No. If they had done so, they might not have left that building alive either, but joined the girl on the floor with a bullet in their necks.

But Arthur finds that answer doesn't satisfy him. Perhaps he should have fought, even if it meant danger, even death.

Perhaps it would have been for the best.

9.35 p.m.

It's nearly time to go, and Arthur pulls on his jacket. It is a warm night. The faintest glow of red from the sunset still glimmers over the western horizon of the city.

He opens his desk drawer, tears a strip from a sheet of letter paper. He tears it in half again, and again, and, closing the door to his room, slips the paper between the door and the frame.

He does exactly as Lockhart has told him.

He does what Lockhart has told him, because he changed his mind in the end. There is one condition, though, that Arthur has been careful to make.

'I need someone else,' Lockhart had explained one night, in his room at the Elite. 'I need someone neutral, not attached to the Embassy, well, not officially anyway.'

'What for?' Arthur had asked.

'We've been approached by two Latvian officers. Now, you know the Latvian regiments are under Red control.'

'What of it?'

'Well, these two aren't playing the Bolshevik game anymore. They want us to help them. They want independence for their country, not Bolshevik rule. If we help them, they'll work with us to stage a counter-revolution.'

'And we give Latvia independence when the Bolsheviks have been toppled?'

'That's the idea.'

Arthur gritted his teeth.

'So where do I come in?'

'I'm not asking much, Arthur. But I can't afford to be seen with them. If there are any Cheka agents watching . . . But there's no reason why a British journalist shouldn't run into a couple of officers in a bar for a drink and an interview, is there?'

Arthur hesitated. Inside he felt nothing. He felt dead. Dead already. He remembered the young prostitute in the anarchist's hideout, and shook himself. *That* was death, not what he was feeling inside. What he was feeling, he told himself, was confusion. The feeling of not knowing, of being lost.

'All right,' he said, 'what do you need me to do?'

'Meet me at the Finland bar, the night after next. You know it? Good. Meet me there at ten. Then I'll tell you where the Latvians have told me to be. You go and meet them instead, bring them to me. Without being followed. Clear?'

Arthur nodded. He didn't speak for a long time,

then put a hand on Lockhart's.

'I'll do it. On one condition. When I meet you at the Finland bar, I want you to have a passport out of here for me, and . . . '

'And?' asked Lockhart.

'For Evgenia, too.'

'My God, Arthur! You can't be serious. You want to elope with Trotsky's secretary?'

'What's wrong, Robert?' Arthur said. 'I thought you of all people would understand.'

Lockhart sighed, admitting defeat.

'You mean Moura? Yes, I do understand. I understand completely. I'm besotted with Moura, there's no other word for it. I have found someone who makes me happy. You and I are the same Arthur, the only difference is that you may be able to get a divorce and marry your Russian girl, whereas I am a member of the establishment. Divorce is out of the question, never mind marrying a Russian. My wife back home in England is a woman to whom I proposed after we'd had just one dance together. I made a mistake. But I'll pay for that mistake always, whereas you may be free to try again.'

He forced a thin smile.

'But it's not that easy. I don't doubt you love Evgenia, but where will you go? She won't be allowed into England; she's a Bolshevik.'

'I've thought of that. I'll go to Stockholm. It's still neutral; there's lots of British, Russians, White and Red there. We can live there until the war ends.'

'Oh, and when will that be?'

Arthur smiled despite himself.

'Soon, Robert, soon.'

Lockhart frowned.

'What you're asking, Arthur . . . It won't be easy.'

'Nevertheless, do it for me and I'll help you.'

There was another long silence, then Lockhart whispered.

'Very well. A passport. And I'll arrange everything for Stockholm. But you'll have to clear a way out of Russia with the Bolsheviks.'

That night Arthur lay in bed, and his conversation with Lockhart took him back to that short spell he'd spent in Stockholm, as beautiful as Petrograd, perhaps even more so, and with a sense of safety that had fled the streets of Russia long before.

He thought of the two wealthy English children who he'd amused by pretending they were Russian peasants for an hour or so, and as he did so, it seemed that it had been a lifetime since he wrote that book.

Will I ever write another? he wondered. *Or will I be doomed to write a journalist's lies for the rest of my days?*

A lifetime, a lifetime.

Oh, Tabitha.

What have I done?

9.35 p.m. continued

So Arthur made his condition with Lockhart, but there was still the small matter of getting the Bolsheviks to agree to let him across the border. As an Englishman he knew he couldn't travel through Germany or Finland, but there was an option open to him.

He went to the Kremlin, to see Radek, to strike a deal.

'It seems to me,' he said, 'that the Bolsheviks could use a contact in Stockholm.'

Radek nodded, in his hobgoblin way.

'Indeed. That city is the key to the West for us. But we have Vorovsky there. What could you do for us?'

'An English journalist to disseminate news from Moscow . . . Does that not give you something you do not currently have?'

Unusually, Radek was reticent.

'I'll think about it. Come back tomorrow.'

'But . . . '

'I said, come back tomorrow.'

Time was starting to run out, Arthur knew, but

when he returned the following day, he was not to be disappointed.

'Very well, Comrade Ransome. You will travel as a diplomatic courier to Stockholm. I for one am sorry to see you go. You are the finest example of your nation it has been my pleasure to meet.'

Arthur smiled modestly at the compliment, and slightly surprised by it, almost missed what Radek said next.

'Good luck, Comrade Ransome. Oh! One more thing. Comrade Trotsky would like to see you before you go.'

The name alone was enough to scare Arthur now. Now he'd seen what he was capable of.

'Why does he want to see me?'

'Oh,' Radek said, 'merely to wish you well.'

It crossed Arthur's mind that it was very unlikely that Comrade Trotsky, Commissar for War of the new Soviet State, would take the time to wish him a safe journey, but there was no choice.

He was walked from Radek's office to Trotsky's by a couple of Red Guards.

Trotsky rose to greet him, and then bade him sit in a chair across the desk from his own.

He studied Arthur slowly, as if deciding how best to berate a small child. Arthur was too nervous to utter a word, but noticed with amusement a small hole in the window, just like the one in the Smolny, back in Petrograd.

'Mr Ransome. All is well?'

Arthur nodded.

'Come now,' Trotsky said. 'Do we not know each other? Can we not speak freely?'

It was all Arthur could do to stammer one word.

'Yes.'

'Excellent. Then you will agree with me that all is well. That Miss Shelepina is safely appointed as of this morning in her new position as secretary to Comrade Vorovsky and will soon be on her way to Stockholm.'

Arthur froze in his chair.

'Yes, of course if you are to leave then Evgenia must go too. Do not think I am so heartless. Or so ignorant of the facts . . . '

He let his words sink in for just long enough, then went on.

'Yes, she will be safe from the Whites. Safe too, from the British who are pretending they haven't invaded our country at Murmansk, yes? So all is well, and I think you can agree that we have been very helpful in arranging all this for you. And maybe I will be safer, too. Miss Shelepina had an accident rather similar to my own.'

He nodded at the bullet hole, and laughed a hollow laugh.

'It seems she is no better with firearms than I am.'

Arthur nodded, dumbly, though his mind was racing, trying to stay out of trouble, trying to keep ahead of the game.

'I understand that Radek has given you some papers

to deliver in Stockholm. I also understand you have agreed to publicise news from Moscow once you are established there, news that may help people understand what we are about in Russia. For that we are grateful, but you know, we have people abroad already. You understand that. We have people working for us, in Stockholm, in London and so on. They are good people, but they are short of one thing. A necessary evil to do the work we need.'

He paused and pulled out a small case from underneath the desk. It was such a funny looking little case, Arthur was struck by it immediately. It was dark green leather, with thick crimson straps, and brass buckles and corner pieces. Trotsky fiddled with the catches.

'They need money, and we need some way of getting it to them.'

He spoke on, but Arthur didn't hear a word, because by now Trotsky had opened the case and displayed its contents. Inside was a scene from a child's picture book, a fairy tale, where the hero not only wins the princess's hand, but the glittering treasure too. Inside the case lay far more jewellery than he'd ever seen in his life. He saw diamonds, ropes of pearls, rubies and gold, but only for a few moments, as Trotsky slammed the case shut, and pushed it towards him.

Arthur snapped from the spell.

'About three million roubles worth,' he said. 'That's the answer to the question you have in your mind. And here's a receipt for it. All you have to do is sign the receipt, take the case, and give it to our man in Stockholm.'

Arthur desperately tried to weigh up everything he'd seen and heard. Could he *dare* refuse Trotsky? And what if he did what he wanted? Then, surely, he would be a traitor.

'Are you telling me to do this?' Arthur said, eventually.

'No, I am asking you.'

'But if I don't do it. What then?'

Trotsky shrugged.

'I will find some other way.'

That wasn't what Arthur wanted to hear. He wanted an assurance that he wouldn't have put himself in danger; he didn't give a damn about how Trotsky got his Red gold to Sweden.

He took a deep breath, and stood. With a pounding heart he reached out for the case, and slid it back across the desk towards Trotsky.

'Then find another way.'

9.40 p.m.

Arthur walks down the staircase at the Elite Hotel. It is twenty to ten.

There's some kind of commotion in the lobby, a gaggle of people surrounding someone, raised voices. Arthur's seen it many times before, he knows what it means. News, or more often, the rumour of news, from the Revolution, from the war with Germany, and lately, from the war against the White army, faithful to the Tsar.

He draws level with the crowd, not intending to waste time, when he overhears two words.

'They're dead!'

He stops, and despite himself, loiters at the back of the crowd.

'Murdered!'

'Good riddance,' says a voice. 'They deserved it.'

'Maybe *he* did . . . but the whole family?'

'Did they ever show any concern for you when you were starving? No!'

And that is how Arthur hears that the Tsar, and the

Tsarina, and all five children have been executed by Bolshevik guards. The rumour is that the White army was closing in on Ekaterinburg, where they were being held. A decision was taken to shoot them before they could be rescued. Arthur wonders who made that decision? Some fanatical captain, power crazy, in Ekaterinburg? Or someone in Moscow, Lenin maybe, or Trotsky, who only this morning told Arthur not to think him heartless?

He feels sick at the thought of the murder of the children, but puts his head down and slips away from the crowd. He's hurrying past the doorman's office, but cannot see little Kashka anywhere. A need to see her strikes him, a need to have her ask her question, and for him to give his usual answer, but this is a ritual he will have to forego tonight. It seems like an omen.

Arthur walks into the night air.

Ten seconds after he leaves, another man leaves the lobby. He follows Arthur down the street, though some way behind, on the opposite side.

Arthur, head down, doesn't see him.

Damn! He looks at his watch. Having had hours to get ready, the drama in the hotel has made him late.

It's five to ten, and he picks up speed, but without resorting to a run. He mustn't draw attention to himself.

Not tonight.

He thinks about the Tsar's family, trying to imagine what those final moments were like. Did they know what was happening to them? Did they scream? Did they die quickly? It's too awful, and it makes him even more determined to go along with Lockhart's plan. He's seen how calculating the Bolsheviks can be on more than one occasion, but something nags at him, making him feel sad for some reason. A few more steps and he knows what it is; it's that life for the Russian people was even worse under the Tsar. But does that make it right to murder children?

No, he tells himself, it does not.

But what would he rather happened?

What should happen now?

He wonders if anything he or Lockhart or anyone does will have the slightest effect. For some peculiar reason, he sees the country as a huge bear, a great Russian bear, running loose, under no one's control.

Meanwhile, the figure behind follows doggedly, but Arthur senses nothing. He turns into smaller and smaller streets, heading for a dead part of town that's even more lawless than the rest of Moscow.

He's going to be late, but he can't help that. He glances at his watch and then as he lifts his gaze he sees himself reflected in the grimy glass of an abandoned shop. Something moves in the corner of his vision.

He crosses the narrow street, doubles his pace, turns a corner and immediately ducks into a dark doorway, ears burning for the sound of footsteps behind him.

He's right.

A second after he's pushed himself out of sight in

the doorway, the figure who's been following him walks past.

Arthur steps out smartly behind the figure and taps him on the shoulder.

The man turns.

Arthur wags a finger.

'Robert! You'll have to do better than that.'

Lockhart sighs briefly and then laughs.

'At least now you'll have to believe I've been listening to you,' Arthur says.

'All right. Very good,' Lockhart admits. 'But we shouldn't be seen. We're nearly at the Finland. Come on.'

They duck under the low archway to the bar without pausing, and head straight for a table in an alcove.

Arthur slides onto a bench with his back to the wall while the Scot orders a bottle from the waiter.

'Vodka?'

'What else?' Arthur says.

Lockhart pours a three-finger glass of vodka and shoves it across the table to Arthur.

'Wonderful stuff,' he says. 'Cures all manner of ills. You can see why they invented it.'

Arthur smiles and drinks half of it at a gulp. It's cheap stuff and it burns his throat, but he's pleased. It's what he needs, to go through with what he's decided.

'Ready?' Lockhart asks.

Arthur's mind races. In an awful few seconds, a host of images and conversations from his years in Russia jostle for supremacy in his thoughts. They all want something from him, something *of* him. Buchanan. Lockhart, who holds the key to Arthur and Evgenia's escape; a passport that will get them into Stockholm, but only if he gets what he wants. Howard and Vorovsky, in Stockholm. He sees Trotsky and Lenin, the Jew and the Russian. He sees Trotsky pushing that green case across the desk towards him. He sees all the people he's ever known in Russia; he sees the great bear, running loose and wild through the forests and plains of Russia. He thinks of the Tsar and his wife and children, he thinks of Ivy, and Tabitha. He hears Evgenia, sees her and tastes her kiss, as if she were there before him.

The visions in his mind wrestle with each other, and argue and fight, creating a din that it seems will never end.

He cannot stand the noise of their chaos, and only when there is silence will he consent to speak. With a supreme effort of will, he banishes them all.

Lockhart is staring at him.

'Arthur? Are you ready?'

'Yes,' says Arthur, then, 'no. No, I'm not ready.'

Lockhart's hand hovers over his own glass, mid pour.

'What . . . ? Here, have some more vodka.'

'No, Robert. I'm not scared, I'm just not going to do it. I'm sorry. I'm sorry to let you down, but I'm not going to do it.'

Lockhart grabs Arthur's arm across the table, not aggressively, but it still hurts. There's a look in Lockhart's eyes that Arthur has never seen.

'You told me you'd agreed. You said you'd do it! You can't change your mind now.'

'I have changed my mind, Robert. You talked me into it. You're a persuasive man, you know. But it's not for me, what you asked. It's not my affair.'

He stops, but Lockhart is still too angry to speak, so he goes on.

'Have you heard the news?'

Lockhart shakes his head, gently.

'What news?'

'They've murdered the Tsar. All the children.'

Lockhart nods.

'So, that's even more reason to try and topple them, isn't it?'

'No, Robert. It isn't. It's even more reason to stop interfering. This is nothing to do with us. All the time I've been here I've been arguing for British involvement, British help for Russia, and all the while our government has been dithering about whether to ignore the Bolsheviks or invade the country and get rid of them. I've argued against it. I thought Britain should leave well alone, but I've been every bit as guilty of wanting them to interfere. I wanted Britain to help Russia beat Germany, to end the war before my brother gets killed. I wanted my own result from it all, like everyone else. The truth is, we should get out of here, and leave them to sort their own problems out.'

'But Arthur, we've always interfered. When the war started, we interfered. When Rasputin became a problem, we interfered . . . '

Arthur held up a hand.

'You're telling me we, you, had something to do with his murder?'

'Not me. But our people . . . played a part. I don't know it all myself, but that's not the point, Arthur. You can't let me down, let your country down.'

'That kind of talk is useless, Robert, don't you see? I'm not going to get involved in anyone's schemes. There's a bigger story going on in Russia, far bigger than us, one that may not end in our lifetimes, and I know my place. I'd forgotten it, but my place isn't on the British side, or the Russian one, but in the middle. In no man's land.'

Arthur stops, and is surprised that Lockhart doesn't leap down his throat, but instead, sighs, and lets his head hang.

'Dammit, Arthur,' he says. 'Why do you have to be right?'

He swigs his vodka.

'Why do you always have to be right? I only wish I had the strength to say no, too. To refuse to play the whole bloody game. But then, that's what I'm paid for. To play the game.'

He smiles bitterly, and somehow Arthur knows he's thinking of Moura.

'Isn't there anyone else who can meet the Latvians for you?' Arthur asks.

Lockhart looks at his watch, calculating how much time he has to play with.

'Yes,' he says, 'Yes, there is. I could get Reilly to do it.'

'Sidney Reilly?'

'Another of our agents. Could have asked him in the first place, but I don't like him. I don't trust him to get it right. The man's a fantasist.'

'It's a simple enough job. You said so yourself.'

Lockhart smiles.

'Maybe. Maybe. I'm going to have to find him then. I don't have long. Goodbye, Arthur.'

He stands up, and as he does so, Arthur sees his chance of leaving Russia about to disappear through the door, but Lockhart pauses, and moves his hand to his pocket.

'Here,' he says smiling. 'Have your damn passport. Evgenia's on there too. I'd do the same thing with Moura if I could. Not going to step in your way.'

Arthur grabs Lockhart's hand and shakes it.

'Don't say a word,' Lockhart says. 'Not one word, you hear? Now get out of here. And Arthur . . .'

'What?'

'For God's sake. Be happy. The two of you.'

Part Three

A Fairy Tale, Ending

Сказке конец

1

And how much do we ever know?

How much do we ever know of our own stories, as we live them?

I thought I knew what I was doing, and why. Or should I say, who I was doing it for, but life is never that simple, and with hindsight we sees our lives laid out behind us and we think; God damn me to Hell, I was a fool.

2

The moments of our lives are like the leaves on a tree, each one separate but each connected to the branch, each branch to the tree itself. The young green leaves dance and rub as the wind blows through them, but when the autumn of our life arrives, they wither and fall to the ground in a jumble. But now, at least, they're still, and we can walk down from the house and look at them, pick them over and try to make sense of it all.

We left Moscow, and escaped to Stockholm, and I thought it was all going to be easy, but how quickly everything began to fall apart.

To fall apart.

I'd left Lockhart in the bar that night, so sure of what I was doing, so sure I was right to turn him down, but soon such certainty crumbled.

And I became a spy, after all.

3

The going was hard, saying goodbye was harder. We had to travel separately, Evgenia and I. She travelled with Vorovsky, overland. They'd been given permission by the German government to go by train via Berlin and then to Sweden. All too soon she was gone and I wondered when I would see her again.

Meanwhile, I travelled posing as a Soviet courier. The Bolsheviks furnished me with some papers, and gave me the protection of a Latvian guard, who was to translate my Russian into, of all languages, English, for any border officials. It was an irony that might have delighted me, but I was too nervous to enjoy any such frivolity.

I got to Stockholm safely enough, but then things began to blacken.

Evgenia was not there. I had thought she would beat me, having left first, but day after day went by and there was still no word from her. I called at the Bolshevik Embassy regularly, asking if they had news of Vorovsky's party, but all they could tell me was that they had reached Berlin.

183

With every day that passed I grew more and more worried. And, with every day, more questions were raised, but there were no answers.

I needed to work. I had strung the *Daily News* along, and they were growing impatient. I needed to start writing for them again, regularly, or they'd pull the plug and I'd be back in London before Evgenia ever made it to Stockholm.

I went to the British Legation to talk to Sir Esmé about whether I could be allowed to telegram from Sweden, which was, after all, neutral territory, but something had changed. No one smiled, no one welcomed me. Even Sir Esmé, whose children I had once entertained, dealt with me in an offhand manner.

I held my peace for a while, and was rewarded by permission to resume life as correspondent for the *Daily News*.

There was a condition however. While I was discussing the matter with Sir Esmé there was a knock at the door and in came an officer. It took me a moment to recognise him.

'Ransome,' he said, holding out his hand.

Then I remembered; Major Scale. The last time I'd seen him was in Petrograd, in 1917.

'Major,' I said. 'How can I help?'

'It's I that can help you, I think,' he said.

'We're going to get you back at work, Ransome,' Sir Esmé said. 'Sending your reports. To make things easier, you'll give them to Major Scale and he'll have them telegraphed for you.'

'To make things easier?' I asked, slowly.

'Yes. To make things *easier*. And more . . . secure. Major Scale is with the Intelligence Service. Your communications will be more secure this way.'

'I see,' I said. 'From who . . . ?'

Scale lost his temper then and told me I was bloody lucky to be allowed to send anything anywhere, but Sir Esmé soon told him to be quiet.

'It will be better for everyone this way. That's all.'

I agreed, with no further argument. I'd just have to be more careful about what I said, that was all. It meant I'd keep my job, and be able to stay in Stockholm. I went back to the small house I was renting, out on the sea lanes at Igelboda, and brooded, thinking about Evgenia, about where she might be, and what she might be doing.

A day later I found out why the mood toward me had soured. It was Lockhart.

As I learnt what had happened, my heart beat fast and light.

Damn it, I remember thinking. Damn it, damn it.

Damn me.

God damn me for a fool.

The first I heard was a rumour on the street that Lenin had been assassinated. It had taken a few days to reach Stockholm, but the British Legation had obviously known about it for days. As soon as I heard I ran to see if they had further news.

Sir Esmé showed me an imported Russian paper, which had arrived that morning.

A young Jewish woman had fired two shots at Lenin at point-blank range. He was still alive, but badly wounded, perhaps fatally. He had taken one bullet in the lung, the other in the neck, and was in a coma. He was alive, but his chances of surviving were less than good.

There was more news, from Petrograd. Two days earlier the head of the Cheka there had been assassinated. There had been riots and the British Embassy was attacked. Cromie, our naval attaché, who had once given me a flag with which to claim an embassy, had resisted the intrusion and, after killing a Cheka commissar, had been shot dead.

Another man I counted a friend, gone.

Meanwhile in Moscow, and later the same night as the attempt on Lenin's life, Lockhart and his second-in-command at the mission, Hicks, had been arrested. Lockhart had been accused of masterminding a massive plot against the Bolsheviks.

Sir Esmé nodded at the Bolshevik newspaper in my hands.

'There,' he said, 'what do you make of that?'

The newspaper made lurid work of the story. I knew ninety per cent of it would probably be lies, but that meant ten per cent was true, and which, I wondered, was that ten per cent? The 'Lockhart Plot' accused

186

Robert of plotting with anti-revolutionary forces to kill Lenin and Trotsky, to set up a military dictatorship, and of planning the destruction of numerous railway bridges in order to bring Petrograd and Moscow to their knees through starvation.

It had all been a trap. There had been no Latvian officers, or if there had been, they had no intention of defecting to the anti-Bolshevik camp. It had been a honey trap, and Lockhart had walked straight into it.

And I had nearly followed him.

I swallowed hard and at that moment did not dare look Sir Esmé in the eye. I had never mentioned to Evgenia what Robert had wanted me to do. She'd been ill, and besides . . . Besides, I admitted to myself, there was still the question of loyalties. Her loyalties. Not for the first time it crossed my mind that perhaps I was being taken for a fool, and that, if I *had* told her, I might now be in the Kremlin too.

I stared at the paper, pretending to read, but taking none of it in. The words blurred before my eyes, and swam across the page, but then I saw another name I recognised. Reilly.

Sidney Reilly figured in the accounts of the plot, too. I had never met him, but Lockhart had told me about him. Could he have dragged Robert into something that was nothing to do with him?

The same thought had obviously occurred to Sir Esmé.

'Lockhart's no murderer,' he said. 'Nor in the business of paying people to murder on his behalf.'

'No,' I agreed, though did he know, as I did, that Lockhart was a spy of some sort.

'Indeed, Ransome, but then, people are not always what they seem.'

Involuntarily, I smiled. How many times Lockhart had told me the very same thing.

'Is something funny?' Sir Esmé asked.

'No, not at all. I just . . . ' I paused. 'Sir Esmé, what you say is true. Sometimes people are not what they seem, and I think I may be a victim of such thinking.'

'Really? How so?'

'It seems that since my arrival in Stockholm I have been under suspicion. I don't know why. Though I might guess.'

I threw the paper onto his desk.

Sir Esmé pushed his chair back and came round the desk to me. He perched on the corner of it and spoke quietly.

'And *if* you were to guess, what would you say?'

'I would say that people are suspicious of me, because I know the Bolsheviks. I have spent time with them. That much is true. I even like some of them, though others are more small-minded than it's possible to imagine. And I think that because I left Moscow immediately before they were all arrested, it's thought that I had something to do with it, or, at the very least, that I knew about it and did nothing to warn my friends, my compatriots. That's what I'd guess.'

'Very well, you have said it. And I may tell you that you're right. That's precisely what people are saying, and since you've worked this out, then why shouldn't I join them and think it the truth?'

'Because I did nothing!' I said, too loud. Sir Esmé tried to shush me. 'I knew nothing about the invasion of Archangel, and that's why the Bolsheviks had all the British in Moscow arrested. How could I have known about that when even Lockhart didn't know it was going to happen?'

'Fair point.'

'Yes, it is. And furthermore, do you really think that had I known everyone was going to be arrested that I'd have said nothing to him? Robert is my friend. I told him the show was over, but that was only my opinion. All I meant was that I was leaving. He knew that.'

He stood again, silent for a time while I tried to calm down. Anger would get me nowhere.

He turned back to me and smiled, though it was thin and unconvincing.

'I want to believe you. To be honest, I don't think you have it in you to lie about something like this.'

'Thank you,' I said.

'There are some who wouldn't think it was a compliment.' He laughed. 'To survive in this game you need to be able to practise deceptions of all kinds.'

'Maybe so. But I don't count myself as part of this game.'

He seemed affronted.

'Is that so? So you're above the rest of us are you? A journalist's independence perhaps, free of concern for anything but a story and a good headline.'

'That's not the case.'

'No? Where do your loyalties lie, Ransome? To Britain? Or to the Bolsheviks? Or just to yourself?'

I stood. There was no point arguing. And though all I could do was worry about Evgenia, I *could* help Robert.

'No,' I said. 'There are people I care for. People who have died, and I could do nothing about it. I've lost people too, and it was my fault. Now I can't be with them. But there are still those I love, who I will protect for all I am worth.'

'That's a fine speech,' he said, and as I met his eyes I knew he was being honest. 'But what are you going to do?'

'I'm going to save Lockhart's skin. If I can, and then maybe you'll know where my loyalties lie.'

4

I wrote a long telegram to Radek, asking, urging, begging him to see that Lockhart's execution would serve the Bolsheviks nothing. Would only distance them from contact with the Allies. They already had Cromie's blood on their hands; I urged him not to add to the list of the dead.

Even as I wrote, I knew one thing. I knew that the telegram would be intercepted and read by the British Intelligence Services, and I knew it would only confirm their opinion that I was a friend and accomplice of the Bolsheviks.

But I didn't care. I couldn't care, not while Robert was rotting in some cell in Moscow.

I sent the telegram.

Then, there was nothing to do, but wait.

5

The leaves on the tree were rustling.

The strands of my life were rubbing against one another.

I can see that now, now that the years have rolled on, the leaves have fallen and I have had a chance to pick over them as they lie on the ground.

I was waiting.

The days dragged by, and I sat on the porch at Igelboda, watching the sea lanes, watching and waiting for boats to come in. I smoked my pipe, and I wrote letters home. It had been months since I had heard from anyone in England.

It was so very lovely, that view from the porch, across the bay, but I never saw it once, not until the day I heard footsteps on the gravel path beside the house.

Evgenia saw me the same moment I saw her, and dropped her bags.

She ran to me laughing and all I could do was laugh back at her.

'What?' I said after a while. 'What happened?'

She laughed some more.

'I didn't hear a thing from you,' I said. 'I had no idea . . . How did you know I was here?'

'Arthur, it's been such a journey. We were stuck in Berlin for weeks. Then finally we were off. But I sent you a wire to say I was coming.'

'I never got it,' I said. 'My God, I've been so worried.'

I held her tight to me again, laughing tears of relief and of joy, then leant back from her slightly, my hands on her hips. I stared deep into her eyes. Something in them spoke of the distance there had been between us; the time we'd been apart. It frightened me. Even though the distance and the time had vanished, the fear that I might have lost her for ever lingered in me.

'But how . . . ?'

'How did I know you were here?'

She smiled.

'Arthur, you think you are so unimportant, that no one could be bothered with you, but you are the talk of Stockholm; the mysterious Englishman who arrives from Red Russia . . . And besides which, I went to the British Legation and they told me where to find you.'

Now it was my turn to smile.

'I needn't have worried,' I said, 'you are far too clever to need me to worry about you.'

'Maybe,' she said, 'but I like you to worry about me. Oh! I forgot, there was a letter waiting for you at the Legation. Here.'

She fished in her coat pockets and pulled out a

slightly crumpled envelope.

'It's from England,' she said, as if that were something ever so suspicious.

'It's from my mother,' I said, as soon as I saw the handwriting. 'Do you know this is the first letter I've had from her since January.'

'I like the house, Arthur,' she said, looking at the garden and the bay beyond it. 'We can make this our home, but first, we are on our honeymoon!'

She went over to her cases, laughing to herself, looking over her shoulder at me, and smiling. It was perfect. *She* was perfect. Unable to take my eyes off her for long, I watched as she picked her things up and brought them up to the house.

I opened the letter.

I was about to read it out loud, but the words died in my mouth. There are moments when you see that something awful is about to happen, and there's nothing you can do about it, something terrible that you want with all your heart to be a lie, but you know it's the truth.

I only had to read a few words of Mother's letter. *My Dear Arthur. I'm so sorry. To have to tell you . . .* I read no more, but dropped the letter onto the wooden boards of the porch and stared out to sea.

'Arthur!'

Evgenia saw me standing like a statue and held my hand, then saw the letter on the floor.

'Arthur? What is it? Arthur?'

'My brother,' I said. I could hear my voice as if someone else were speaking, hollow and dry. 'My brother is dead.'

6

I don't remember much of that evening, nor of the following day.

I was wounded by the news, struck dumb for hours before I could respond even to Evgenia's urgent pleas for me to say something, anything, at all.

The war had taken Geoff at last, as I had always known it would. The war took my friends, and now it had taken my brother, killed somewhere in France. Only when I finally had the courage to pick up the letter and read it to the end did I learn the final bitterness.

He had been killed in January. I had not known. It had taken me over half a year to find out that my brother was dead, because no single letter had made it to Russia. And all that time I had been hurling my pointless letters out into space, to my mother, asking her to wish Geoff well, to send my love to him. All those hopes and wishes, spent on someone already dead. My heart was too sore then to admit that maybe I would send my love to him, even though he was dead. I know now of course that I will always send my love to him.

Wherever he is.

7

The response to my telegram from Radek was not reassuring. It was impossible to recognise the hobgoblin's usual wit and education in the perfunctory reply he gave me. He said that Lockhart was indeed being held in prison and was only not being shot to avoid giving the Allies easy propaganda.

I took a small crumb of comfort in this. If Lockhart's name was enough to make the Bolsheviks unwilling to shoot him, that wouldn't change quickly, and the fact that Radek had replied to me at all was a good sign; it meant they might be open to negotiate on Lockhart's release. If I had heard nothing, I would have feared for Lockhart surviving more than a couple of days.

With this in mind I went to see Sir Esmé. I proposed a bargain, a deal we could make with the Bolsheviks.

'Do you know of Litvinov?' I asked.

'A little,' Sir Esmé said, 'what of it?'

'I know him. Quite well. Lockhart knows him too, he gave him a letter of introduction to Trotsky when he came back out here. And we have him locked up in Brixton prison. I suggest that we propose a straight swap; Litvinov for Lockhart, and whoever's being held with him.'

'Well, it's only him now. That's the latest news. He and Hicks were arrested, then both freed. But Lockhart was arrested again by some goon named Peters. They've moved him from the Loubyanka Prison to the Kremlin.'

Peters. That made sense. I thought of his boot rolling the dead prostitute over, and his chillingly banal words. *Perhaps it is for the best.*

The first prison Sir Esmé referred to was in the building the Cheka used as their headquarters in Moscow, an old insurance office at number eleven Lubyanka. I didn't know the place but I knew the Kremlin jail as something else entirely. It had a dreadful reputation; the story was that no one who'd ever been imprisoned there had left alive.

'There's something else, too,' Sir Esmé said. 'Since you're his friend . . . Our people in Moscow say they've arrested his mistress, too. Her name is Moura Budberg. Maybe you know her?'

'Yes,' I said simply, and for once I was no longer surprised at what they knew. They knew everything, it seemed. 'Yes, I know her.'

'But that's besides the point, I'm afraid. Our concern is with our man. Ransome, I like your plan. But *I'll* talk to Whitehall about it as if it were my scheme. If it comes from you they'll imagine a Bolshevik scheme. You get in touch with Moscow and sound them out. Nothing definite at this stage, right?'

'Right,' I agreed. 'I can talk in generalities.'

'One thing before you go. If I suggest this, I need to know it might work. Do you think the Russians will go for it? We're not in one of your fairy tales now.'

'The Bolsheviks have many faults,' I said, ignoring his cutting remark, 'but they're a practical bunch. They love talking and sometimes they like doing deals. I think it's our best bet.'

'I hope you're right, Ransome. For Lockhart and for you.'

I walked over to the house used by the Bolshevik Legation to meet Evgenia, but was told she had already left for the day. Officially she was working as Vorovsky's secretary, but after their nightmare journey the kind old Russian seemed to be letting her have a chance to settle into her new home.

I left Stockholm and caught a tram out to Igelboda. As I got on, I noticed a man in a suit get into the rear of the car. Something bothered me and I realised I'd seen him earlier on, outside the Bolshevik Legation. I decided I was being paranoid, and to forget about him, but when the tram got to my stop, I stayed on and ran all the way down to Saltsjobaden. From there it was a fair walk home and I set off briskly. Once or twice I was foolish enough to stop and turn round, but could see no one. I laughed at myself for my imagination and went home.

Back at Igelboda I found Evgenia. As she made some supper, I told her what had happened and what Sir Esmé had said. All the time, though, I knew that something had changed in me. As I heard myself talk, another part of me explored the feeling that had swept into me.

I felt I'd been living in limbo, at least since my arrival in Sweden, maybe for months before. Geoff's death had been a final terrible blow, and had pushed me over the edge into a blackness that would have killed me if only it hadn't been so cowardly.

I had left Ivy. Yes. I had lost my daughter in one way, and my brother in another. That was something to be sad about, but not to stop living for.

I'd been letting things happen to me, without making a fight, without struggling for what I wanted, but finally, finally, the action of actually doing something to help someone, had freed me.

For a short, clear evening, everything seemed so simple.

I had found a woman I loved and who loved me, and I knew that I was going to do everything I could to protect that.

8

For how long did I forget I was a writer?
It must have been months, a year, or more.

But Sir Esmé's remark about living in fairy tales reminded me that once I had written a book, a good one, that had been praised and that children had loved so much they read it from cover to cover and then started at the front again.

I thought of my *Russian Tales* and realised I no longer owned a copy of my own book. I wondered if I could ask Sir Esmé to let his children just show me their copy, even once. So that I could believe I had written it, that it was not some other fantasy of my own devising.

I remember thinking about the time I'd written it. It was a happy time. I was in love again, not with a woman, but with Russia; war and Revolution had not yet engulfed me. I remember, in an early draft of the *Russian Tales*, I had decided to kill the grandfather at the end of the book. A bear comes pounding out of the woods one day, apparently for no reason, and knocks the old man down. The children are sad, so very sad, of course, but I was trying to show that pain passes, they would grieve, but they would then grow again, and become adults; so that they no longer needed anyone to look after them.

I showed that early draft to the friends I was living with, in the house in the trees near the banks of the Volkhov, and they were dismayed.

'You can't do that!' they protested. 'You can't kill their grandfather!'

I made my case, but they would not be convinced.

'No, no, no,' they said. 'It's not that kind of book. It's a happy book.'

And in the end, I took their advice, and brought Old Peter back to life. That's something you can do as a writer, you have that power, and during the time in Stockholm, I was glad I had done so. Death was all around me, and I was glad I hadn't added to the list, even in fiction.

Grandfather lifted himself up from the snow where the bear had knocked him, dusted himself off, and he lived. He lived, and now, being a character in a book who has survived to the final page, he lives forever.

But even in my book of fairy tales, little Maroosia and Vanya have no father and mother. I knew then that if I ever found time to do another book I would never again write a story about a small girl without her father. I knew then there'd be children having adventures, and maybe with some real danger, but they'd be laughing and smiling, and coming home in the evening to their mother and father to have hot chocolate by the fireside.

9

It wasn't long before my own fairy tale unravelled a little more.

Genia and I enjoyed our Swedish honeymoon, I relaxed a little, and into that space our feelings for each other were able to grow.

My telegrams to Moscow worked, and we heard that Robert was to be released at last. I had earned the trust of the Intelligence Services, and the respect of Sir Esmé, if not of those who strode the corridors of Whitehall, back in London.

It was around then that Wyatt, another agent, made his silly proposal, and silly though I found it, in the end I agreed.

But I am getting this all wrong, because the first thing that happened was Lockhart's arrival in Stockholm, on his way home.

After the dust had settled and Lockhart had made a round of official meetings, we went out for dinner, just him and me and Evgenia. We found a bustling place in the Gamla Stan, and put ourselves in the corner, away from view. We spoke in Russian for Evgenia's benefit, and Robert told us his story.

'You look well, really,' I said, though in my heart he looked years older than when I'd last seen him only a few months before.

'Liar,' he said, but he grinned. 'The food was . . . not great.'

'I should think not,' I said.

'Potatoes and soup,' he said. 'Every day. Though Peters told me it was all they had to eat themselves.'

'Peters!' I said. 'That rat.'

Lockhart shrugged.

'Arthur, I don't know what's what any more. Would you believe me if I told you I have a letter in my possession that Peters has asked me to deliver? To his English wife, when I get home!'

'English?' I asked, amazed.

'Remember what I always say . . . '

'No one is what they seem. I know, but . . . '

'Listen, Arthur. I owe the man no favours. I've spent the worst month of my life thanks to him, but there's always more to know about someone than you might think. I'm not sure he's the monster we all thought he was. He told me he feels ill every time he signs a death warrant.'

I laughed bitterly.

'And that makes it all right, does it?'

'No. No, I suppose not. But I can't hate him anymore. He was the only person I saw every day in the prison. He tried to make me as comfortable as he could. When there were idle moments we talked. About England, about history, about his wife. He misses her.'

Lockhart stopped, and took a drink, his thoughts suddenly far away. There was one thing I hadn't dared ask him yet, though the answer was, perhaps, obvious. So very obvious to Evgenia and me, as we sat across the table from him; a table for four, with only three present.

We let him talk.

'Don't let me drink too much tonight,' he smiled. 'Miss Shelepina, you'll make sure I don't overdo it? It's been a while since I had a drink. But why am I asking a Russian for help with temperance!'

We laughed, Evgenia frowned, and then we waited while a waitress brought our food. When she had gone, Robert continued his story.

'I can't tell you what it was like, not properly. The rooms they gave me in the Kremlin were comfortable, but small. They were some kind of internal apartment, the only windows opened onto corridors outside. There were guards at each window constantly, who changed every four hours, and who woke me up all through the night. But I slept poorly anyway. I was worried out of my mind. Peters played with me, I think. He showed me all the papers, the Russian ones, full of stories about me, about how I would be tried and executed. One day, I was taken for some exercise in the yard, and the guard, who was Polish I think, told me they were having a bet. Two to one I'd be shot.

'And then there was Moura to think of . . .'

Again Lockhart stopped. He pushed his untouched food away and pulled his wine glass closer, filling it from the bottle at our table. He offered it to us then, but we both shook our heads.

'They had me in solitary, but Peters told me Moura was locked up with the rest of my mission in the Butyrsky jail. Every day I begged Peters to let her go, to let them all go. Whatever I might have done had nothing to do with them, I said.'

'But you'd done nothing!' I exclaimed.

Lockhart put his glass down, and stared at the table.

'I'm afraid,' he said in English, 'that's not entirely true.'

'I . . . what do you mean?'

'Nothing important,' he said, this time in Russian once more. 'Miss Shelepina, excuse my manners. Anyway, after a week or two Peters told me that Moura had been released. The relief was enormous. Peters was in a good humour. It seemed that Lenin was getting better; he would probably pull through. That made my position a bit safer. If he had died, I wouldn't have given tuppence for my chances.

'A day later and he brought me a package from Moura. She'd sent me clean clothes, the first I'd had for days, some food, even coffee and ham. And a pack of playing cards. The clothes and food were welcome, but it was the cards that stopped me from going crazy. I played patience all morning.'

'And what of Lenin, now?' I asked.

'Shh, Arthur,' Evgenia said, gently putting a finger to my lips. 'Don't interrupt.'

'The last I heard before I left he was sitting up in bed. Peters told me the first words he said were "stop the terror" but I think that's just a nice Bolshevik story.'

'Is the terror real?' I asked. 'I didn't want to believe it. I hoped it was Allied propaganda.'

'They may have exaggerated it,' Lockhart said, 'but I'm afraid it's true. I saw it with my own eyes. Before they moved me to the Kremlin I was in a room in the Loubianka with a window that looked down onto the courtyard. I saw the executions myself. Three Tsarist ministers and a priest on my last day there.'

I shook my head sadly.

'I know, Arthur. I know what you're thinking. But this is a war. It might not be as clear as the one against Germany, but Russia is at war with herself now. You always were too kind-hearted. I'd say naive, but that's unfair. You're a dreamer, Arthur. A visionary. You champion the underdog whether he's right or wrong, and I'm afraid that ultimately the Bolsheviks are just dogs like the rest of us politicians. It's not about good or bad, though we like everyone to think it is. It's about power.'

'You're right of course,' I said. 'It's just that it's the individual who suffers. People like you. And Moura.'

Lockhart nodded.

'Guess who made exactly the same point to me about

a week ago,' he said. 'Peters, of the Cheka. Yes, I know it's crazy. But it's true.'

I raised an eyebrow.

'I know. I know. But let me tell you this about Peters. He may be a ruthless killer, but then he does extra-ordinary things. One day near the end he came into my cell. He announced that it was his birthday, but said that since he preferred giving presents to receiving them, he had brought me a present. He opened the door and called down the corridor and Moura came in. Nothing else could have been a better present. Peters wouldn't leave us on our own, but sat on my chair and began to reminisce, in the way that you do on your birthday. He talked about his life as a young revolutionary. He'd been locked up, tortured and so on, but I wasn't really listening. My heart was in my mouth, because Moura, who was standing behind Peters, did an incredibly dangerous thing.

'She'd been standing fiddling with the books I'd been allowed to have. She caught my eye, and then pulled a piece of paper from the top of her dress. She slid it into the top book on the pile. If Peters had seen . . .'

'What did you do?'

'I nodded to Moura, ever so slightly, to show I understood,' Lockhart said. 'And then. My God! She hadn't seen me, so she took the paper out and repeated the performance. I started nodding like an epileptic. Somehow Peters was too lost in his story to notice me.

Shortly after, he stood up and took Moura away again. I waited for them to go then rushed to the book to find the note. Six words, that was all. "Say nothing. All will be well."'

'She risked her life to put your mind at rest,' Evgenia said. 'How great is love!'

Lockhart smiled, but it was a sad smile.

The story did not have a happy ending.

He told us of his final days in the cell. Of his release. He'd been given two days to pack and leave. He told us of his final evening with Moura, and as he did so, my heart bled for him. Under the table, I held Evgenia's hand as Lockhart told us how he'd had to tell Moura he was leaving, and how dignified she'd been.

'I understand.'

That was all she'd said.

He knew he would never see her again.

We were all silent. The waitress came and cleared our plates, brought us coffee, which Lockhart clung to as if it were a lifeline. Evgenia excused herself and went to the bathroom. Lockhart stared into the deep brown swirls of coffee in his cup.

'Do you know,' he said after a while. 'The most ridiculous thing of all. At the end, after Peters told me he was going to let me go. He offered me a job. Can you believe that? He wanted me to become a Bolshevik.'

I didn't know what to say.

'And do you know what, Arthur? I was bloody tempted. Just to be able to stay. With her.'

10

I shall never forget Lockhart's story.

Nor what he told me before he left for home, for England.

What he told me in the Finland bar and that night in Stockholm showed that the Bolshevik claims about him were not unfounded. I wouldn't have believed it if I hadn't heard him say it, but it seems that in his last few months in Moscow, he had changed his mind about the situation in Russia.

Whenever I had spoken to him before he would always agree with me about the British policy towards the Bolsheviks, but behind the scenes, he was doing what his government wanted him to do. He'd secretly been collecting money from the rich White Russians, money that was being used to fight the Bolsheviks. He said he'd been lucky that the Cheka were as stupid as they were terrifying, or they'd have found a lot more evidence to use against him. The night they burst into his flat he had the coded book he'd once shown me in his pocket. It was obvious he was going to be searched, and in desperation he asked to use the toilet before they took him away. They agreed but wouldn't let him close the door. A guard stood with his back to him, and Robert did the only thing he could think of. Page after page of the incriminating note book he used as toilet paper, and if he hadn't, then maybe he'd never have left the Kremlin alive.

I saw him off at the station.

'I've had enough of the spying game,' he said. 'It's no way for men to be.'

'What will you do?' I asked.

'Go back to England and try to repair my ruined career. And my marriage, too, if I can. But first I'm going home. To Scotland. Home for me is where the rivers run north.'

I wrote in my reports about what Lockhart had told me. Not everything of course, but what I knew I was supposed to say. I told of the Red Terror, and the Cheka, and Lenin's recovery.

And I continued to write my stories, though deep down I still felt I wanted to write something for children. I was sick of revolution, and of the adult world. Children go on and on, and the thought of Tabitha's easy happiness made me want to write a simply stunning book for children like her.

Then, one day in November, the war ended. We heard the news straight away; it spread like wildfire across the city in a matter of moments. That evening I walked by myself down to the bay and lit a pipe.

I'd been sent some good black tobacco by Gardiner at last, and I puffed away furiously to keep out the cold. In seconds I was taken home. I was in the snug at the Hark to Melody, drinking beer with old friends, long since dead. Then I was talking to charcoal burners in the woods above Coniston Water, and then on the mining train to Millom.

So the war was over. I thought of the doorman and his daughter.

How many times had she asked me her question? How many times had I answered it; soon, soon. But of course, I realised abruptly, the war was not over in Russia, not yet. There were still battles to be fought.

I smoked some more.

Russia had got under my skin, I knew, but despite everything it had failed to change me. I was the same man I was all those years ago when I ran away to escape from Ivy.

And yet, as I stood watching the ships slip from the harbour in Stockholm, and followed the glow of their tail lights as they drifted between the low line of rocky hills, out to the Baltic, and then to Russia, a lump stuck in my throat and I was overwhelmed by a desire to follow them.

11

Be careful what you wish for, it may just come true. The world war may have been over, but peace had not spread everywhere. There was war still in Russia, civil war, and if Evgenia and I thought we were free of it, we were mistaken.

Stockholm was flooded every day with refugee White Russians, bringing with them stories of the horrors of the Bolsheviks, of Cheka reprisals, and of starvation and cholera. Pressure was growing on all sides for the Swedes to expel the Bolshevik delegation from their city and, early in the new year, they did.

Vorovsky and his whole party would return to Moscow, and Evgenia with them; since Britain's borders remained firmly closed to her.

I had a choice; go home to England without her, or follow her back to Russia, into its red heart.

I thought of Robert, saw his face as he spoke of

leaving Moura behind, and knew that there was only one way open to me.

That's when I went to see Wyatt at the Legation, and talked of his silly plan once more, and that's how I became S76, British agent, and headed for Moscow.

12

It was a long and epic train journey and with every mile my fear grew. The coaches rattled like the rhythm section of a jazz band drunk on its own beat, and though Evgenia slept, I could not. All I could find was fear. It had seemed so easy to become S76 in Stockholm, and be drilled in an agent's methods, but now it was real, and we were approaching the lions' den. What if I'd been watched by Bolshevik spies? What if they already knew about me? I felt as if the word was written in inch high letters on my forehead.

Spy.

Our first night back in Russia my dreams were not easy ones.

Towers rose on all sides, the great onion domes of St Basil's, in all their various many-coloured patterns. At first I admired them, then horror grew in my chest as the towers multiplied and pressed in around me, growing so high the sky was obliterated. The ground fell away beneath me and I tumbled like Alice into a space that had no end. I woke, panting in the dark, and sleep was hard to come by after that. When finally it did return, I was assailed by more and more bizarre dreams and woke early, having dreamed I'd been riding around Red Square on Trotsky's back, while unseen assassins fired pot-shots at me from their Mausers.

But my worries were unfounded, and though Trotsky was wary of me, and evidently thought I was a spy, I was rescued by Lenin himself, who told Trotsky not to be so suspicious of an old friend of the Bolsheviks.

I spent a harmless couple of months preparing material for the *Daily News*, and for the Secret Intelligence Service too, of course, though it was pretty anodyne stuff.

Life settled down; for form's sake Evgenia went to live with her mother and sister, who had moved to Moscow, and got a new job in the Department of Education.

We fell into an everyday routine.

One day, two American journalists came to see me, asking that I accompany them on a mission to London with a set of Bolshevik peace proposals. Bullitt and Steffens had been sent from Washington to gather information about Russia. Having done so, they seemed to think that the Allies would listen to them more seriously with my first-hand experiences to back them up.

I agreed to go. It would be a good chance to go home for the first time since before the October Revolution. I could see Tabitha, Mother, and the Lakes. Evgenia was safe, and happy, and I had no fear of any difficulties in getting back into Russia; I was in favour with both the Bolsheviks and some of the British authorities, at least.

Evgenia was unsure about me leaving at first, but I explained that I wouldn't be gone long, and that if the peace proposals were listened to, the war in Russia might end, too.

'All right,' she said, at last. 'All right, but Arthur, one day I want us to be together. For always.'

I nodded, and pulled her into my arms.

'I know,' I said. 'One day. Soon. We'll find a way to be together. We'll find a way.'

So I left Moscow, and travelled with the Americans across Finland and Sweden and Denmark and eventually to England, though if I had known then what was going to happen, I would never, ever have left Evgenia.

13

Tabitha.

What a superb child. On the way back to England with the Americans I thought of little else but her. What would have happened to my daughter since I had last seen her? How much would she have changed in eighteen months? I remembered that previous visit clearly, every moment of it. It was back when Russia had been about to throw herself into the second Revolution of 1917, though I knew nothing of it at the time.

What did Tabitha say, that day?

What did she do?

Yes! She ran out of the gate the moment she saw me.

'Daddy!' she cried, and flung herself at me.

'You're so tall!' I said, laughing.

'Daddy!' she said, moaning, 'why do all grown-ups say that?'

'You're right. I'm a bad grown-up and I won't say it again. Ever.'

'Promise?'

'I promise.'

That was one promise to Tabitha I kept. Though there were others, whispered into the dark air above her sleeping head, that I did not.

At tea she gazed at me as if I was a creature from another world, and to be honest I felt like one. I was intensely aware of the triangle between the three of us. I wanted so much for Tabitha to like me, not to hate me for going away, but I didn't want to do anything to upset Ivy, who was in as good a mood as I could remember.

After tea Tabitha pulled out a penny whistle and begged me to play her favourite tune, 'The Lincolnshire Poacher'.

I obliged, and obliged twice more, until finally I suspected Ivy's patience might be wearing thin.

'Think what you'd like to do tomorrow,' I called softly as Ivy took her upstairs.

'I will!'

I sat and watched the fire for a long time, my mind drifting pleasantly, until finally Ivy came back down.

'She seems happy,' I said, idly.

'She *is* happy, Arthur,' Ivy replied.

'Yes, of course,' I said quickly. 'I only meant . . . '

'What?'

'Well, of course I don't see her so very much.'

'No.'

'It's just that she seems to cope with it all. Very well. With my not being here.'

Ivy looked at the fire, her face showing no emotion.

'She wasn't yet three when you went. She doesn't know any different.'

She was silent and I knew I had been rebuked. I opened my mouth, then shut it, deciding to take my punishment without complaint. It would be better that way. For everyone. And besides, deep down I knew she was right.

There was a long silence.

'I'll go and tuck her in,' I said, and before Ivy could reply, I hurried up the stairs.

I knocked quietly on Tabitha's door, which stood slightly ajar. Getting no reply I pushed the door gently on its hinges and stole into the darkened room. I could hear Tabitha breathing deeply and dared to rest on the edge of her bed. I listened to her snuffles for a while, then put my hand out and stroked her head.

'Daddy might be coming home,' I whispered. 'Would you like that?'

I left the words hanging in the air, wondering if they would find their way through her sleep and into her dreams.

The evening passed easily enough, and Ivy chatted about this and that. By the firelight I thought she looked as beautiful as when we'd first met, in London, all those years ago. We'd had fun then. It was a wild time, bohemian and poor, but happy. When did it go wrong? We'd been through a lot together. There'd been the libel trial, when I was sued over the biography of Wilde I'd written. I won, but the pressure had been enormous.

Was it when we moved to the country? Maybe life was too dull for her. Maybe that's why she'd had to invent all the nonsense that she did.

We talked on and reminisced about our days in London, and with a shock I realised I was enjoying myself. It was a shock, because it was the last thing I had expected.

Eventually, I began to yawn and decided to turn in for the night.

I made my way upstairs.

I passed Tabitha's room, and then paused briefly at the next door, which stood open. That had been our room. I mean Ivy's and mine. It looked the same as ever, but it was not mine anymore. I moved on down the corridor to the guest room, and in the dark, I undressed and slipped into bed.

Next morning I was woken by Tabitha jumping on the bed.

'Daddy, wake *up*! It's *so* late!'

I rolled out of bed and forced my eyes open, then fixing Tabitha with one eye, pretended to fall back asleep like a plank hitting the deck.

She laughed, tugging my hands to pull me up.

'Careful, you'll have them off!'

I sat up and made Tabitha a deal.

'Let me have a bath and then we'll do whatever you want. Agreed?'

'I want to go and lie in the grass in the sunshine and sing songs,' she said. 'It's a lovely sunny day.'

I looked out of the window.

'Yes, it is. But it's also November, and I think lying in the grass may not be a good idea.'

I raised a hand to silence her protests.

'However, we can go for a walk and dance and sing songs instead.'

'Hooray!'

'That's a yes, is it?'

'Yes, it is,' she said. 'Now do get in the bath, Daddy.'

'Yes, Miss.'

Tabitha made a very solemn face.

'And do wash everywhere, won't you?'

I took my bath and ate a quick breakfast, informing Tabitha that I had indeed done my duty and laid right down in the bathwater. On the sideboard lay a stack of newspapers that I had ordered. I made out the word 'Russia' in a headline and leant across to pull it over, when I caught Ivy's eye. She looked from me to Tabitha, who was already putting her shoes on, and with an effort I pushed the paper back into place with the others.

I finished some toast, pulled on my boots and made for the door.

I turned. Ivy stood by the table.

'Coming?' I said.

She hesitated.

'Come on,' Tabitha said. 'Just a little walk.'

'Bring the camera,' I added, and Ivy nodded.

She smiled.

We walked up the lane and saw that Tabitha was right. It was a lovely sunny day, and we were easily warm enough without coats. Tabitha took my hand and began to dance about, lifting one leg and then the other like a demented sailor.

I danced too, laughing and singing a song I made up on the spot. It wasn't very good but it made Tabitha giggle and once she'd started, Ivy couldn't help joining in.

'Here,' said Ivy. 'Let me take a photograph. Arthur, help me set it up.'

I took the camera from her and still dancing like a lunatic fiddled with the iris and shutter settings.

'That should do it,' I sang, and rejoined Tabitha under the big oak at the top of the hill.

'I want a photograph of us dancing!' Tabitha declared.

'You'll have to keep still,' Ivy called. 'You'll come out all fuzzy if you're moving like that.'

'Right, Tab, you've got to pretend to dance, get it? Or the camera will get confused. That's it, one leg in the air. Wait for me. Okay! Ivy! Quick!'

We just about held on while Ivy took a shot, then collapsed on the ground, laughing ourselves silly.

'Let's dance again,' Tabitha said. 'Please?'

'No more!' I protested as we picked ourselves up. 'No more for now. But just think, in the photograph we'll always be dancing.'

'That's true,' she said, thoughtfully, and suddenly she seemed much older than her years. 'I hadn't thought of that.'

On the way home, we picked up sticks and branches from the woods to have a fire. We were nearly at the house when I turned to see Tabitha dragging a massive branch, as long as she was tall.

'Here, Babba,' I called, 'let me give you a hand.'

Tabitha turned round.

'Don't call me Babba, either!' she said, so seriously I didn't know if she was joking or not.

She grinned, stuck her tongue out and ran into the house, laughing.

There and then I cursed myself a hundred times. How could I have done it? How could I ever have left her? She was delightful, funny, and pretty. But more than that she was my daughter, and I, her father, had all but left by the back door when she was asleep.

I never wanted to leave her, but it didn't stop the guilt, and feeling like a bad dog, sick to my bones, I slunk into the house.

That evening, as I tucked Tabitha into bed, she held my hand.

'Daddy?'

'What is it?'

'Are you going to stay for ever?'

'It's not that simple,' I said, and already hated myself.

'Why not?' she asked, not cross, simply innocent. But she was right; why wasn't it that simple?

'Some things are complicated, and one of those things is my job. I may have to go back to Russia.'

'Is it very far to Russia?' she asked.

'Very far.'

'Farther than London?'

'About a hundred times as far. Across the sea and across the land.'

'Oh,' she said.

'But listen, Tab. I'll always be your father, and I'll always love you.'

'I'll always love you, too.'

'Goodnight,' I said, quickly kissed her forehead, and left.

I went downstairs and picked up the newspapers, and read about Russia, so very far away.

14

What a farce it all was!

That whole episode with the Americans, that trip home, the first in eighteen months. Once again my mind had been occupied with seeing Tabitha, seeing Mother, and England, and I'd been blissfully unaware of the nonsense going on behind my back. It was only years later that I learnt some of the details. How someone in London had given orders to the Finnish police that I be arrested if I tried to cross their borders, and that I should be locked up in a Finnish jail, without informing the local British Embassy. How I travelled with Bullitt and Steffens, as one of their party, so the Finns let me through, unaware of who I was. How the Finns then arrested the agent tailing me, locked him in a jail cell without informing the local British Embassy, and refused to believe his protestations that he wasn't Arthur Ransome.

Even when I got to England the farce didn't stop. The Secret Service lost track of me once or twice, as I crossed Scandinavia and caught a boat to Newcastle, though when I got to King's Cross I was approached by a plain-clothes man and asked to accompany him to Police Headquarters.

At Scotland Yard, I was being grilled by the Chief Superintendent, a man named Thomson, when the phone on his desk rang. He listened briefly, opened his mouth to say something, thought better of it, then put down the receiver without saying a word.

'That,' he said, with a heavy sigh, 'was our man in Newcastle.'

'Really,' I said.

'Yes,' said Thomson. 'He tells me that Arthur Ransome will be arriving on a boat in Newcastle tomorrow . . .'

'I see,' I said, and grinned.

Thomson sighed again.

'Bloody, bloody fools,' he said, and then laughed.

With the ice broken, Thomson dropped the hard-man routine. We talked about fishing for a while and then he told me I was free to go. I found him a charming man.

I went to see my mother, who was down in Kent, recovering from an eye operation. She was well, in spite of a nasty bruise lingering around her eye, but that was the moment when I realised she was old. We talked about Geoff, but strangely found there wasn't much to say. Over a year had gone by since it had happened, and over six months since I'd found out, and the pain had crept away into a dark corner inside us both, I think.

'If I had lost both of you . . . ' was all she would say.

'It's good to see you,' I said. 'To be home.'

She smiled.

'But where is home for you, Arthur? It's not here in Kent, is it? It's not with Ivy anymore. With Tabitha.'

I winced, but didn't deny it, because she was right.

'The Lakes,' I said, firmly. 'The Lakes are my home.'

'The Lakes,' she echoed. 'Then what of Russia? What of your Russian lover?'

If Mother had been unable to see my letters, I knew then that someone must have read them to her.

'What about her? Is your home not with her?'

I hesitated.

'It will be,' I said. 'I will go back to her and then . . . I don't know. I don't know. But the Lakes will be my home again, one day. They have to be.'

She slipped her hand from under mine and rang a tiny bell on the tray beside her.

'I hope so, Arthur,' she said, 'and I hope I'm there with you, but remember, home is where you can be with the one you love. Now, do you want some tea?'

I went to the Lakes, and saw some good, old friends. And I saw friends of the human kind too who were delightfully disinterested in dead Tsars and Revolutions.

Summer was coming early and I walked for miles

above Windermere and Coniston, the heavens above my head and the earth beneath my walking boots. I thought of Evgenia often, and smiled, but one day I tried to picture her face, and with shock realised I couldn't.

I sat on a rock, brooding. Coniston Water lay stretched like a silver finger in the early evening light. It was an utterly beautiful landscape, serene, and perfect as only nature at a distance can be. Back in Moscow the streets would still be filthy and the river reeking as it always was in Summer, yet here the day was mild, and the air fresh; the whole world was green and blue. Moscow would be grey, and red. I tried to imagine myself there, and failed. Then I tried to imagine that I had ever been in Petrograd, either, and to my surprise, I failed again.

A chill spread up my spine as I tried to remember that I had *ever* lived in Russia, that I had ever been there, that I knew Robert. Or Evgenia. I came closer to home and tried to remember that I had ever been happily married, that I had ever loved Ivy.

I failed it all.

Then with a cold hand descending on my heart, I tried to believe that I still had a daughter, a happy little thing called Tabitha.

And I failed.

When I came off the hills that night I went straight to my room and packed my case. Next day I caught a train south, to London, and then another out to Hampshire, to see my daughter.

15

Comings and goings.

It had been a long trip already; leaving Evgenia in Moscow, the pointlessness of Bullitt and Steffens' mission, seeing Mother, walking in the Lakes. And now to Hatch.

The last contact I'd had from Ivy was a letter in Stockholm. It had been a reply to one of mine pressing her for a divorce, and it had been, unsurprisingly, a fairly uncompromising letter. But I needed to see Tabitha.

It had been so long, but though I felt the time like a huge gulf, Tabitha was as pleased to see me as ever. I had to work hard to keep my promise not to say how tall she'd grown.

I bit my tongue, and smiled at Tabitha.

'Here. I've got you something.'

From behind my back I pulled out a long, and very thin parcel that I'd brought with me.

'If you can't guess from the shape of it,' I said, 'I've obviously bought the wrong thing.'

Tabitha looked as if she was racking her brains, but I could see she was teasing me.

'What can it be? I wonder, I wonder, I wonder . . . It's no good, I'll just have to open it.'

She laughed, pulling the brown paper from around the segments of the fishing rod.

'It's a small one, but a proper one,' I said. 'We can go down to the river tomorrow and try it.'

Tabitha smiled.

'All right,' she said, looking at Ivy. 'Is that all right, Mother?'

Maybe it wasn't the best idea. But Tabitha did seem to want to go fishing. We went down to the Little Nadder, and it was a fine summer day, warm as you could wish for. I showed Tabitha how to use the rod, and how to be silent. We pushed out on the water, in a hired boat, letting the boatman guide us to what he thought would be the best spot.

'It's very important to be quiet,' I said, 'and you mustn't let your shadow fall on the water, or the fish will know you're here.'

She nodded, and I showed her how to thread a worm onto the hook. She pulled a face, but she did it without fuss.

We fished. Tabitha caught minnows, and I caught nothing, until finally I conjured up a huge pike, which I pulled snapping into the boat.

Tabitha shrieked, and the boatman grabbed the fish. He tried to stun it, but messed it up, and then took a long time clubbing the pike until it stopped moving.

Tabitha buried her face in her hands and howled; I was about to tell her it was all right when something surfaced in my memory, something about a small boy hearing the screams of a hare after his father had winged it.

'Take us in,' I said to the boatman, and we went silently home.

I stayed at Hatch another day or so, and as much as I wanted to spend time with Tabitha, I had to leave. It was doing no good, anyway. On more than one occasion Tabitha had caught Ivy and me arguing about the divorce, the final time standing quietly in the doorway of the kitchen for God knows how long until we saw her.

I knew then there could never have been a solution for Ivy and me. And as for Tabitha, I could be a better father to her from a distance than I could under the same roof as her mother. Maybe. Or maybe that's wishful thinking. Either way, the facts were unaltered.

So I went, and once again, made my farewells to my daughter. This time, though, something had changed. In the past, the sadness had only been mine. Now, I saw it tinged Tabitha too, like the touch of a disease. And for the sadness of this sickness I knew there was no cure.

No cure, just the palliative of love.

I put my arms round her and held her.

'Love you,' I said.

'Love you too,' she said back.

I forced a smile, and so did she, and then I went.

16

The worst happened.

The worst. And I knew I should never have left Russia.

Gardiner, my editor at the *Daily News* for so long, lost his job. I heard a rumour from a friend with connections that Lloyd George himself had been responsible. He disliked Gardiner's opinions, and leant on the Cadbury family who owned the paper. Whatever the reason, with Gardiner gone, I no longer had a job either. With no job, I had no reason to be allowed passports, or visas to Russia.

With growing desperation, I spoke and wrote to anyone I could think of who might be able to help get Evgenia permission to leave Russia, but with no success.

Time turned, I saw summer come and go, and I was not a step closer to being with her.

And when I thought things were bad enough, they got worse.

News from the east started to arrive in England. The situation in Russia was bad. Bad for me, bad for Evgenia. The White armies, far from suffering the defeat Lenin had crowed about in March, had increased in strength, and were pushing hard against Trotsky's Reds. With growing support they had started to win a few battles, and now were victorious on all sides.

Admiral Kolchak's armies held Siberia, Yudenich was threatening Petrograd and Denikin had defeated the Tenth Red Army in the south.

His goal now was Moscow.

The papers everywhere were full of the imminent fall of the Bolsheviks.

I ate little, I slept less.

If the Whites took Moscow, I knew what the result would be for Evgenia. There would be no mercy for the Bolsheviks, or those who had helped them. In the meeting with Peters I'd had in Moscow, he'd shown me photos of White Army atrocities; Red Army corpses with their noses cut off, or decapitated.

When the Whites caught Lenin and Trotsky, there would be no mercy at all.

And whatever she might be now, Evgenia had been Trotsky's secretary.

For days that turned into weeks I struggled in vain, until finally I couldn't stand it any longer.

If I couldn't get Evgenia out of Russia, I would go in and find her, and nothing was going to stop me.

17

I had a problem; I might have decided to go back to Russia, but I still had no way of getting there. The *Daily News* was a closed door; since Gardiner had been sacked the views of the paper had shifted from mine, but I needed a job badly, and I got one. I had a call one day from C.P. Scott, the editor of the *Manchester Guardian*. He'd read some of my pieces, and needed a new Russian correspondent. He offered me the job, and what swung it was probably the fact that his son, Ted, had been the closest thing to a best friend I'd ever had at school.

Now I had a reason to go, but I still needed official permission. Once upon a time I'd had contacts in the Foreign Office, but no longer. While I was away in Russia new faces had arrived, old friends had left. My options were limited, but I pestered everyone I could, and in the end Basil Thomson of Scotland Yard managed to sway things for me.

I went to see him the day I collected my papers. I was eager to go, September had come, and the cold weather would soon arrive in the Baltic, and in Russia too.

'Just one condition,' Thomson said.

'Which is?' I said, trying not to be goaded.

'I've been told you can have your visa on the condition that you write nothing untoward for the *Guardian*.'

'Untoward?' I said. 'What's *untoward*?'

'Well,' he said, smiling slyly, 'that's for you to decide. I might tell you that there are some people who have only agreed to you going at all because they think you'll be less of a nuisance in Russia than here. But as to what you report, you need to use your own judgement.'

'And if I make the wrong judgement?'

'Don't,' he said. He wasn't smiling and I got the message. Behave, or else.

Later that day I headed to King's Cross. As the cab pulled in I was vaguely wondering what dramas might occur at the station. Another plain-clothes man? Was I still being followed everywhere?

I had already paid the driver and was halfway across the station yard before I realised how quiet the place was. There were a handful of people drifting around aimlessly, a few porters and guards standing in clusters, chatting, but doing no work. And it was quiet; no trains. No trains at all.

I collared a guard.

'No coal, is there,' he said. 'Nothing running today. Probably not tomorrow. Who knows how long it'll last.'

I shook my head. I'd heard there was a coal strike on but somehow I hadn't made the connection with trains. No coal, no trains.

'But I have to get to Newcastle,' I said, 'urgently.'

'Urgently, is it?' the guard said. 'That's as maybe, but there's no coal. Is there.'

'So what am I going to do?' I complained, not really expecting an answer.

He scratched his head.

'Listen, chum, I've got a cuppa waiting. Now clear off to the docks, you might just catch the Newcastle steamer.'

'The steamer? Of course!' I cried. 'What time does it leave?'

The guard looked as the station clock.

'Midday. Hope you find a fast cabbie.'

It was nearly quarter past eleven.

I ran from the station and threw myself into the first cab I could find.

'The docks! As fast as you can. Please.'

The cabbie laughed, I wasn't sure what was so funny, but I didn't care, because he set off at a good pace. As we went I tried to avoid the torture of looking at my watch every minute.

'I've got to catch the noon boat,' I explained. My driver seemed unmoved. I tried something that usually worked in Russia. 'Double your speed and I'll double my fare.'

That did seem to impress him, and he spurred the

horse on so we were soon heading through the city and out to the docks.

'Do you know where the ticket office is?' I said.

The driver grunted.

'Never mind,' I said to myself. I looked at my watch again. We were almost there, but it was very nearly twelve. I threw some money at the driver and jumped from the cab, bag in one hand, typewriter in the other. The docks spread before me, the river beyond. I could see at least three boats, any of which might be mine.

Desperately I ran forwards, and accosted a steward standing at the head of a line of passengers.

'Newcastle?' I shouted.

He looked startled and waved a hand at the nearest boat.

'Thanks,' I said, and ran off.

'But you can't go aboard!' he called after me, 'Oi! Come back. It's leaving.'

He was right.

As I lurched down the quayside I saw the gangplank being stowed, and a widening gap forming between the boat and the shore.

'Oi!' the steward called again. 'Come back!'

I ignored him, and without thinking, hurled my type-writer and bag across the gap onto the deck, scaring an old lady in the process. She was even more alarmed when I took a longer run up and threw myself after my bags, landing on the deck with a thump. I felt a sharp pain in my ankle, but tried to ignore what it would mean if I had done anything serious.

The gap between the boat and shore had widened further and looking at the water I felt light-headed.

The steward stood on the quay, shaking his head.

'Hey!' he said. 'Have you got a ticket?'

I waved.

'Not yet, I'll get one on board, all right?'

I knew it would have to be all right; they weren't going to turn the boat around just for me. He shook his head, and watched me sail away.

'I have to get to Russia,' I called to him. Then I noticed the strange looks I was getting, and decided it was time to lie low until the boat got to Newcastle.

18

The coastal steamer pulled in to the docks at Newcastle, but, as I thought my luck was improving, it seemed to run out again.

I made my way into the ticket office, and asked about the boat to Norway.

'Ay, lad,' said a boy about half my age behind the ticket desk, 'there's a boat for Bergen. But it's not going anyway. Don't you know there's a coal strike on?'

I smiled and tried not to swear.

'Yes,' I said, 'I was aware of that. I didn't know it applied to Norwegian ships.'

'Ay, well, neither did he, till he got here.'

The boy nodded at a man discussing something furiously with two other men across the ticket hall. He was obviously the captain of the boat, short for a Norwegian, but blond enough to put it beyond much doubt.

I wandered over.

One of the other men turned to me.

'Who are you?' he said, rather aggressively.

'A passenger for Bergen,' I said, and turned to the

captain. 'God dag! Is there nothing to be done?'

Hearing the Norwegian, he smiled and spread his hands wide.

'I don't know.' He shrugged. 'Maybe.'

'The Captain sailed with a half-full hold,' the other man said. 'There's no more than the scraps left, coal dust and rubbish in the ballast. There's probably enough to make it back, but only probably. If he runs out before Bergen . . . '

The Captain was clearly fretting.

'I really do need to get to Norway, as soon as possible,' I said.

'You think so?' he said. 'I tell you I need to get there more than you. It is my wedding anniversary tomorrow. I promised my wife I would be there for once . . . '

He shrugged his shoulders.

'In that case,' I said, 'I think we had better get going. Wives are not people you should upset . . . '

I pulled a face, and he laughed.

'Besides, if we run out of fuel you can burn my luggage. Fair enough?'

'Very well,' he said, making up his mind. He turned to the other men. 'My boat will sail this evening.'

And it did. It was hard going. The coal dust burned badly, and soot billowed from the funnels, raking the decks in black clouds as the wind changed, but I didn't care. I was on my way.

As the packet hauled its way across the North Sea, I tried to talk to the other passengers, the Norwegian and other Scandinavians going home, to see if they knew anything of the news from Russia. But no one seemed to know, or if they did, they didn't want to talk.

I wrote to my mother on the boat, to post when I got ashore. The letter got a bit smudged with soot, but I kept writing.

I have no regrets in my mind. No doubts. I know I must go, I want to go, and if I do not, well, whatever happens it can't be worse than my own guilt if I'd avoided making the journey. So that's that.

I wondered what Evgenia was doing. I guessed she'd be working hard, as usual, but did she know about the advance of the White Army? It was most likely, I knew, that the Bolsheviks wouldn't want to admit that they were in trouble, that Trotsky's Red Army had been losing ground, or that Denikin was marching on Moscow. No, of course they wouldn't be telling the people the bad news, but maybe Evgenia had inside information. I hoped she didn't do anything rash; she was so impetuous sometimes. I tried to keep calm; she'd navigated her way through two Revolutions without my help, after all, and for the time being, Moscow was probably the safest place for her. But I didn't know *what* she knew, for though I had tried to send her several telegrams, I'd heard nothing back from her. I shut my eyes and thought of her, of that evening of Lockhart's party, of that night.

I could only pray she knew I was coming.

I folded the letter and looked for an envelope. I rummaged around the bottom of my case, remembering a small pack of paper and envelopes I usually kept with me when travelling. I hadn't used it for weeks, and as I pulled out the first envelope, I saw something strange.

There was handwriting on it already. A child's handwriting, just one word.

Daddy.

I opened it and inside was a photograph. It was me and Tabitha, and instantly I knew what it was. It was from the visit I'd made eighteen months before, when Tabitha was seven. There we were, on that walk we'd taken down the lane, hand in hand, just pretending to be dancing so the camera wouldn't get confused . . .

I'd left before Ivy had had the chance to get that film developed, and I'd never seen the photo before. It was wonderful. Happy. Tabitha must have sneaked it into my stationery set on this last visit, knowing I would find it sooner or later.

I turned it over. There was writing on the back.

Look Daddy! We'll always be dancing. Lots of love, Tabitha.

I stared at the picture for a long time, and looked at our faces. She was right; in the photograph, we'll always be dancing, always happy.

Then I realised there are actually three of us in it; for although Ivy had been behind the camera, the sun had been behind her. Her shadow leaned in towards us. It didn't matter; it was the truth, all of it. The happiness, the dancing, the shadow. Me, Tabitha, Ivy. All part of our little bit of history, and for once, I felt at peace with it all. Carefully, so carefully, I slid the photograph back into the envelope and put it in my inside pocket.

I needed a talisman, and at that very moment, Tabitha had given one to me.

19

I crossed Norway by train, from Bergen, and then on to Sweden, where I found myself in Stockholm once again. Due to my previous embarrassment there I was only permitted a transit visa, but it was a day or so before I managed to get a boat to sail east across the Baltic to Reval, the fine and ancient capital of Estonia.

And there I was truly stuck.

Not only was Moscow a very long way away, but the opposing front lines of the White and Red Armies lay between me and Evgenia. Estonia had taken the White cause at the outbreak of Revolution; their armies lay locked in stalemate with the Bolshevik forces.

At a loss, I presented myself to the Minister for Foreign Affairs.

The Minister, with the charming name of Ants Piip, made me very welcome. I thought there was every chance he would tell me he had no time for personal affairs, but I explained where I wanted to go, and I explained why.

As I talked he regarded me thoughtfully from under

dark brows, and his face grew more serious as I spoke. When I finished he seemed lost in thought, but then a smile spread across his face.

'You, Mr Ransome, are sent from God! May well you look surprised, but it is true. You are no more surprised than me, I assure you. If I had prayed for something like this to happen it could not have been more perfect.'

'What?' I asked. 'I don't . . .'

'No,' he said. 'But then maybe you are not aware of the current situation with Russia. We are at war with Russia, on behalf of the White cause. But we are struggling. We are a small country, with few friends. We cannot continue this war with Russia, it is killing more than just our men. We want to make a peace proposal to the Bolsheviks, and for their part, the Bolsheviks have made promises to respect our independence if we end the war.'

'So why not simply tell them so?'

'How? The wires between here and Moscow are tapped. If I send a man, an Estonian to Moscow, and he is caught . . . Mr Ransome, if the Allies, and if the White Armies learnt that we want a truce with the Reds, there would be grave consequences. What I need, instead, is an independent man. A neutral figure, someone known by and trusted by the Bolsheviks. In fact I need you, Mr Ransome.'

Then I understood why Piip had given me so much of his time. I was, as he said, the perfect messenger, heaven-sent.

'I'll get you across the border, I'll arrange a transfer to Russian hands for you. Then you can rescue your Evgenia, and I will have my message delivered to Lenin. Do we have a deal?'

I didn't even think about it.

'Yes,' I said, 'we have a deal.'

20

But nothing is ever that easy.

Minister Piip and I might have decided upon a neat little plan that suited us both, but the third party to the equation, Moscow, had not.

At my suggestion, Piip sent a telegram to Litvinov, whose release from Brixton prison had secured Lockhart's freedom. I hoped my old acquaintance there would be enough to get the Bolsheviks to arrange the journey, but it was not.

Piip received a telegram back from Litvinov almost by return. They refused, point-blank, to let me back in to Russia. I don't know what had happened in my absence, but I was clearly out of favour with Moscow. Maybe Trotsky had finally convinced Lenin that I was a spy after all. Which, to be fair, would only be reasonable.

I, however, had other cares, and I wasn't going to be deterred by a mere telegram.

In Piip's office, I told him what to do. I grabbed a sheet of paper and scribbled on it in capitals.

'This is a telegram for Litvinov,' I said. 'Wait three days and then send it.'

I handed Piip the paper and he laughed as he read the five words.

RANSOME ALREADY LEFT FOR MOSCOW

'You are a brave man, Mr Ransome,' he said.

'No. Not brave. Just someone trying to find a home.'

Piip looked at me curiously, but he said nothing.

'So,' I said, 'I'm leaving as soon as possible. Can you get me an escort to the front lines?'

He nodded.

'Of course.'

'And papers? Do you have something for me to take?'

'No,' Piip said. 'You are my message. I cannot run the risk of anything falling into the wrong hands. You will carry your message up here,' he tapped his head, 'which is why only you can do this job. Lenin will believe what you have to tell him.'

I took the night train out of Reval, for Valka. The train was unheated and I froze, getting no sleep at all. Next day I travelled on by narrow-gauge railway to Maliup, where I spent the night with an Estonian captain and his wife. They were hospitable and fed me well, for which I was very grateful.

The following morning, I was taken under escort in a two-horse carriage.

We drove east, but then turned to the south. It

seemed that fighting had broken out again, and my escorts thought I would stand more chance further towards the Latvian border, where things were quieter. The snows had come, and the roads were bad. Progress was slow, but after some hours of driving along idyllic forest tracks, the carriage slowed. It crawled on and on at walking pace for another half hour or so, nothing but trees and snow to be seen, and then stopped.

The escort turned to me.

'You walk from here,' he said in English, and shoved the door open.

I got out, my things dumped in the snow at my feet.

'Our soldiers, there,' said the escort, pointing behind me. 'Russians are there. Good luck.'

With that the carriage made a hasty turn, and then sped away as fast as it could.

I took stock.

It was still morning, and though hints of mist hung over the snowy landscape, the sun was glinting on the tops of the firs and silver birches that surrounded me. As the sun tilted down, the frost on the snow glittered like a certain case of jewels Trotsky had once shown me. That seemed long ago, as I stood on my own in the forest. I looked back to where the Estonian forces were supposed to be, but could see nothing. Was that a hint of something metal shining? It was only a guess. I turned and looked at the way ahead. There was an open field, that led from the clutch of trees where I was standing, over to where the Reds were supposed to be.

Well, I thought. I'm in no man's land. Now what?

In answer to my own question, I pulled my pipe from one pocket, and some tobacco from the other. I risked the cold for a while, pulling my gloves off and holding them in my teeth while I filled the pipe. Gloves back on, I lit the pipe, and began to puff it into life.

No man's land. The space between. The space between one side and another, that belongs to neither. That's where I was. And that's where I had always been, I realised; I'd skirted my way between the Russians and the Allies, but the path I took had always been mine alone.

I relaxed. I was at home here, in the middle of nowhere, and with that comfort, I decided what to do.

I reached down, picked up my bag in my right hand, my typewriter in the left, and began to walk towards the Russian lines.

No one, I told myself, is going to shoot a man smoking a pipe.

If I could have whistled, too, I would have done, but nevertheless I tried to look as nonchalant as possible. As I walked, the minutes went by, and the pipe got hotter and hotter as I clenched it between my teeth, smoke blowing into my eyes.

Somehow I had convinced myself that even the Red Army would understand that a man laden with bags, smoking and walking in broad daylight straight towards their lines could not possibly be a threat.

At that moment, an unbelievably loud bang shattered the peace of the frosty morning. It had been a while since I had heard gunfire, and my heart began thumping even before I had a chance to think.

Then there was a shout, and with relief I knew that the shot was only a warning.

'Stop!'

There was a flurry of snow ahead, very close to me. I'd nearly walked right on top of them. About twenty feet away a man roughly dressed in Red army uniform emerged from a snowy thicket. If he had wanted to kill me, I would have been dead.

He aimed his rifle at me. He seemed unsure what to say, but he knew what to do. He lowered the point of the rifle towards me.

I lifted my bags slightly, showing I would love to put my hands in the air if only they weren't so full. I puffed on the pipe for dear life, showing how incredibly nonchalant I was feeling.

There was a movement to my left and I saw another half dozen soldiers, their rifles pointing in a direction I didn't find amusing. One of them waved me forward. I looked nervously down at my coat. It was the old coat that had seen me through years in Russia, in Petrograd, and away at the front. But it was an old Tsarist officer's coat, and though it bore no emblems or other service marks, I wished I had changed it for something else.

One of the soldiers shouted.

'This way!'

Obediently, I walked with a gun at my back further into Red territory, and very soon we reached their front line trench. Here I was hastily bundled into a dugout, still at close quarters to a rifle.

'Spy, sir,' my escort said.

As my eyes grew used to the darkness, I saw a corporal sitting on a trunk, drinking tea. He looked up, a mixture of boredom and puzzlement on his face.

'Spy? Take him away and shoot him.'

'Wait!' I cried, 'I'm English!'

'Really?' said the corporal, 'and I'm American.'

Things were rapidly going against me.

'I'm telling the truth,' I said, in English, this time, and then in Russian, 'and I'm no spy. I'm going to Moscow. To see Lenin.'

The soldier stared at me for a moment, then burst out laughing.

'Oh! To see Lenin, is it? Take him away and shoot him.'

'Listen,' I said. 'Listen for a minute. My name is Arthur Ransome, and I have an important message from the Estonian government for Lenin. If you speak to Moscow they'll tell you who I am. It's vital I see Lenin.'

The corporal started to sit up.

'Vital? Why?'

'I can't tell you that, but I give you my word.'

'Oh! The Englishman gives his word!' He stared at

me, open mouthed. It was a look of belligerence.

'Try to see it this way. If I'm telling the truth, one phone call to Moscow will settle the matter. And if not, you can shoot me. But if you shoot me before you know the truth, you could be in a lot of trouble.'

He pondered this for a while, and eventually the logic seemed to dawn on him.

'And if you are a spy,' he said, 'I can shoot you then?'

'Yes,' I said. 'Exactly. I promise.'

I was trusting a lot to Moscow, but fortune favoured me.

'Regrettably,' he said, 'we cannot speak to Moscow from here. We will have to take you to battalion head-quarters. That will be best. In fact, then they can decide whether to shoot you.'

'Oh,' I said. 'I see. Good.'

The corporal, now visibly relieved of the burden of having to make a decision, smiled at me.

'But would you like some tea before we go? It's very cold this morning. It's only cherry leaf, but it's good and it's hot.'

21

Almost the same scene was enacted word for word at battalion headquarters.

Once again, my fate rested with the officer I was speaking to understanding that it might be best to ask questions first and shoot later, rather than the other way around, but at last, to my great relief, he agreed to telegraph Moscow.

'Just as soon,' he said, 'as I can find the damn code book.'

He began rummaging around his quarters, looking nothing like an officer of any army, unshaven and badly dressed. When he finally found the leather-bound pocketbook, he held it up triumphantly.

'Ah ha! Now we will get some answers.'

I could only pray they would be the ones I needed, but my luck held, for Moscow replied within hours that I was indeed a journalist, and should be escorted under guard to Moscow immediately. Of my claims to bring a message to Lenin, there was no word either way, but I had done enough, for the moment, to save my skin.

One soldier was all they sent to escort me to Moscow, but one soldier with a gun was more than enough. Besides, they were taking me where I wanted to go. Next day we made our way across open land until we found a railway line, which we walked down, the path being easier hopping from sleeper to sleeper, than sliding through the snow. Eventually, late in the afternoon, we found a small halt, no more than a hut open on one side to the weather, and a small heap of coal. There was a water tank, but it would have been useless for refilling the engine; the temperatures were sub-zero and icicles like white spears hung from the tank.

My guard was not very chatty. I tried to speak to him, more than once, but he was having none of it.

'Is a train coming?' I said, and that was the one question he answered, with a single word.

'Da.'

That at least I was glad of, because I knew we would freeze if we stayed out overnight. Then there was no more conversation, and we sat in the halt. I watched my breath steam out in the freezing air, smoked a pipe and wondered if my life would end by a train track in the depths of the Russian forests. It wasn't something I had planned, but right then it seemed all too possible.

When the train finally came rolling down the track towards us it seemed unreal. In the half-light of dusk, both sound and vision seemed impaired; the train moved slowly towards us like a leviathan from a dream, blowing vast clouds of steam into the air next to us, the wheels slowing and slipping as the brakes brought it to a standstill.

The last silence of the snowy forest lurked behind us, and we clambered aboard. The train jolted into life again, almost unwillingly, but we were away before my soldier and I had even found somewhere to sit.

The train was packed, mostly with soldiers but with ordinary people, too. My guard made some of them move so he could sit opposite me in a compartment. All the while his rifle lay across his chest, as if he expected me to run at any minute. As the journey wore on, however, his mood changed. I think he had finally realised that I wasn't going to try to escape, and I began to chat to him about Moscow, a place, it turned out, that he had never been. Eventually I told him about Evgenia, and then I knew I had touched something in him, perhaps some story of his own, because he listened hard and nodded furiously from time to time as I spoke.

Sometime later an old woman came along the carriage with flasks of tea, and I bought some, sharing it with my guard. We had had nothing to eat all day, and the tea sloshed around inside us, but it was hot. Night came thick and deep beyond the carriage windows, and the soldier fell asleep, still cradling his gun, but now, as if it were a baby.

Finally I slept too.

By mid morning, we were approaching Moscow. All the way, my heart had been beating faster and faster, as I grew more and more apprehensive about what I would find, and whether I might be welcomed, or not.

There was no way out, but somehow that made me feel worse. I had to return to the West. I had to, but only with Evgenia.

As we got off the train, my escort, whose name I had learned was Dragonovich, seemed unsure of what to do.

'You must go and see Lenin?' he asked, as if I was in charge.

'That's right,' I said. 'You should take me to see him. We'll find him at the Kremlin. Here, I'll call a drozhka.'

I trotted out of the station, and Dragonovich tagged along, clutching his rifle and pack and staring all about him at the wonders of the Moscow architecture.

As we approached the Kremlin wall, his mouth fell open. The onion domes and spires of Red Square rose beyond.

'My God,' he said, 'it's so beautiful. And so terrible.'

I nodded. He was right; he had put his finger on exactly what I always felt in Moscow. I took the chance to suggest something to him.

'It would be as well for me to see Comrade Litvinov first. At the Commissariat for Foreign Affairs.'

Dragonovich, still wide-eyed like a child, nodded.

'Yes,' he said, 'very well.'

I breathed easier. It would be sensible to see Litvinov, that was true, but I had another reason for the detour.

We had some trouble with the Red Guards at the gates, but soon we were up into the vast maze of the Kremlin itself. I knew Evgenia might be hidden somewhere in its vast belly; I was possibly very close to finding her now, but had to keep my nerve. I led the way and in a short while was knocking on Litvinov's door.

As I walked in, the old man rose from behind his desk and glared at me. My soldier hovered behind me, completely out of his depth and aware of it.

'Mr Ransome!' Litvinov declared. 'You are a most persistent individual!'

He snatched a piece of paper from his desk.

'Do you know what this is?' he shouted. 'I have just received this, this telegram. From Reval, where the Minister for Foreign Affairs writes to tell me that you are already on your way to Moscow. This despite the fact that I had specifically forbidden your journey.'

I spread my hands.

'There must have been some confusion,' I said.

'So I see. And who is this?'

He turned his wrath on Dragonovich.

'What do you want? Did you bring him here, or did he bring you? Never mind. You have a unit to return to, I assume? Yes? So get out of my office!'

The soldier slunk away, his tail between his legs. I felt sorry for him, I wondered whether he would even manage to find his way back to the station, never mind the Estonian front.

Litvinov sat down. His anger seemed to have left.

'What are we to make of this, Mr Ransome?'

So I told him. I told him about the peace proposals from Estonia, and I think he believed me.

'I will call Lenin and you can tell him this yourself.'

He picked up the receiver of the phone on his desk.

'Of course,' I said, quickly, reaching out a hand to stop him using the phone. 'But would you mind first, to tell me . . . to let me, I mean, see someone else?'

Litvinov smiled.

'So that's it. Love? You would have made a good Russian, Mr Ransome. A very good Russian. Very well. I will phone Comrade Lenin shortly and tell him you are on your way. Of course, the Kremlin is a big place. You might, I suppose, lose your way . . . '

There was a sly look in his eyes and a grin on his face.

'Thank you. Thank you so much,' I said.

'I presume you know which way to lose yourself?'

'The floor beneath this one, on the northern side?'

'Exactly. You have half an hour.'

Even as I left his office I could hear Litvinov asking to speak to Lenin, and I hurried through the high dark corridors to find the Education Department.

I was outside the door, and lifted my hand to knock, then let it fall.

It had been not weeks, but months. We had heard nothing from each other. My heart grew perfectly still, as if waiting to know it could beat again.

I didn't knock, and just walked into the office.

One or two faces I didn't recognise glanced up at me, and I looked blankly past them. Then, there she was. She left her desk and came to me, and in that short space, there was time for tears to roll down her face, and a smile to spread on her lips.

I put my arms around her gently, as if she might break, and she put her head on my shoulder and wept silently.

She stood back, and we were aware of being stared at by the other people in the room.

'Arthur!' she said. She laughed and then tugged both my hands. 'Come here. Come with me. I have something you want.'

Still laughing, she pulled my hands and led me back into the corridor and down the hall.

'Do you remember?' she said. 'Can you guess?'

I began to laugh too, because I had smelled a familiar smell.

'Here,' she said, throwing open a door onto a small kitchen area. A pot bubbled over a portable stove.

'Potatoes,' she said.

'That's what we want,' I said.

I had never eaten anything better, I swear, than that dish of boiled potatoes. My hunger from not eating for two days, and my hunger to be with Evgenia made that dish the sweetest food I had ever had. I gazed at her and she grinned back at me, unable to stop smiling. Her eyes sang.

This is what you want. This is what you want.

Then she stood.

'Oh!' she cried. 'Wait here.'

She hurried from the makeshift kitchen where I sat perched on a stool, but was back moments later clutching something in her hands preciously, as if it were gold, or maybe an egg.

'Here,' she said. 'Dessert!'

She produced the end of a bar of chocolate, about three squares, which we shared, and savoured, ever so slowly.

'Wherever did you get that?' I asked.

'I've been saving it. For months,' she said. 'I've been trying not to eat it. I told myself you were going to come back and that when you did we would share it. But sometimes there were days when I gave up hope. I'm sorry. But I didn't know. On those days, I let myself eat one square. But I told myself that if I ate all the chocolate, you would never be coming back.'

She held up the empty wrapper and screwed it into a ball.

'You came back just in time, Arthur.'

She tried to smile, but she failed and the tears came again.

'I'm so sorry, Genia,' I said. 'I'm so sorry.'

'Never mind, you're here now.'

'Yes. But now what? You know that the Whites are advancing on Moscow?'

She nodded, closing her eyes.

'Yes, we have heard. But Trotsky says they will be defeated.'

'He would,' I said. 'He would and maybe he's right. But what if he isn't? You have to leave, Evgenia. I want you to come with me when I go.'

'Where? Where will you go? Where is there that's safe for us? You can't stay here, even if I could. And I can't go to England. And neither of us can go to Stockholm.'

'Estonia,' I said, 'Reval.'

'But we're at war with Estonia.'

'Not for long,' I told her. 'That's how I got here, I've brought a peace proposal from Reval. Estonia wants peace with Russia, and I know Lenin wants peace with Estonia; it'd be one less part of the White Army for him to fight. Soon, Estonia will be a neutral country, and we can live there. Safely. Only . . . '

'Only what?'

'Well,' I said, hesitating. 'Your mother. Your sister . . . '

'I know,' she said. 'I know. But they know too. We've talked about it. If my Englishman were to come for me . . . They'll be safe, even if the Whites take Moscow; they are not Bolshevik, they are not known as I am.'

'So you would leave? Leave them?'

'I will never leave them,' she said. 'I may leave Russia, but they will always be with me. And Arthur, more than anything, I want to be with you.'

I held her hands but said nothing, because there was

nothing to say. We understood each other, and that was enough.

'I don't have long,' I said at last. 'I have to go and see Lenin. Tomorrow we will leave. You should go home. See your family, and pack whatever you need to bring.'

'All right.'

'But don't bring anything more than you can carry. Easily.'

'But Arthur, how are we going to get out?'

'The way I came in. Across no man's land.'

22

Moscow to Reval.

Almost six hundred miles.

A journey that nearly cost us our lives. Three times.

Of the first part there's not much to say. We finished our business in Moscow, I with Lenin, Evgenia with her family, and I saw little of her as she made preparations to leave.

Lenin was delighted with me.

All he was concerned about was peace with Estonia, but he, like Minister Piip, was not willing to trust anything to the wire, or paper, and gave me a full account of what I was to propose to Piip, which was in short, a peace conference. Of course, for the time being, that left Russia and Estonia at war, and it was that front line which Evgenia and I would have to cross.

'I have read your book,' Lenin said to me. '*Six Weeks in Russia.*'

I didn't answer. Whenever anyone says that to me

about something I've written it seems foolish to say anything until they've said what they thought of it.

'I was disinclined to like it,' he went on, 'but then I had a letter from Radek. You know he is still in prison in Berlin, and he said it was the first thing he had read of the Revolution that brought us Bolsheviks to life, as real people. And so I changed my mind about it. You have done us a great service. If there is anything I can grant you in return, you have only to name it.'

All sorts of outrageous requests flashed through my head, but I let them go.

'I don't think so,' I said. 'Just help us as far as you can to leave Russia.'

'Indeed. I have bad news. There has been another outbreak of fighting on the Estonian front. The fighting is spreading south. Your journey out may be harder than the journey you made to get here. But we will do what we can.'

Then we left, by train, and at first all was well.

We made a slow but comfortable journey of four hundred miles through the day and overnight to Rejitsa, and then on the following day to Korsovka, though this time we sat on the floor of a freezing cattle truck, huddled around a small fire.

At Korsovka we were handed over to the Commissar, where we had a basic but welcome lunch of soup and bread. The Commissar was grave-faced.

'The fighting is everywhere,' he said. 'To and fro, we capture a village, then the Whites take it back. There is no telling where you will be best to go. All I can say is that if you do run into any trouble, sit tight in the first cottage you see and wait to be captured by the Whites.'

And hope they don't find out who Evgenia is, I thought.

He gave us two carts, one driven by a small boy in which we put all our luggage, and one driven by a gloomy old militiaman, who seemed convinced we were heading into certain death.

We trundled out of Korsovka, into the unknown. The boy and I walked at the side of the horse, while Evgenia sat on our luggage. No one spoke.

I'd found Evgenia, true, but we were not safe yet. With every step we moved a little way forward, but I didn't know whether it was one more step towards safety, or danger.

We made our way along forest tracks, deeply rutted and frozen solid. The trees reached silently towards us on all sides, opening out into a clearing here and there, and our carts rumbled on.

Then we heard firing. It was impossible to tell where the shots were coming from, but they sounded distant. There was nothing to do but go on.

We saw no one, but then, long after the shots we'd heard, we saw men running low through the trees. They emerged onto the track ahead of us, and then ran back the way we had come, taking no notice of us at all.

We went on, and another mile or so later we saw a farmhouse up ahead. Outside was a group of people, not soldiers, but peasants. As we came up, I called to them.

'Do you know where the front is?'

They stared at us, and then one of them pointed. Back the way we had come.

At this, the old militiaman turned his cart around, and sped away hell for leather, for home. I looked at the young boy leading our cart. He was chewing on a piece of straw, which he spun from one side of his mouth to the other. I feared for him; he had no business risking his life for ours.

'And you,' I said, 'do you want to run for home, too?'

He shook his head.

'I have brothers on both sides,' he said, 'I'm happy in either place.'

'Thank you,' I said. I was relieved by that, but the peasants looked at us less happily. They were in no man's land, in a civil war. If they were caught sheltering Reds . . .

'We are on our way to Marienhausen,' I said. 'Do you know the way? Is it far? Perhaps we could ask you for some tea before we go on.'

There were five men, and an old woman. They regarded us suspiciously, but the old woman spoke.

'Yes, we can make some tea.'

She led the way into the farmhouse, and we found it was a single large room, dark inside, but beautifully warm; a fat stove roared away. Two small children saw us come in, and ran to hide behind a hefty chair next to the fire. From there they gazed at us as we took out our own samovar to make tea.

Without removing her headscarf, the old woman bustled around the kitchen. Our boy grew brave, and sat himself next to the stove. The children peered round the chair at him, and for a moment I was transported to a different Russia, one that I had made myself, in a book of fairy tales.

Now in no man's land, we could expect that the next soldiers we saw would be White, and I decided to get rid of anything that might endanger us. I opened the door to the stove and fed into it all the passes, letters of safe conduct and every scrap of paper from Moscow, while our samovar came to a boil on top. The old woman watched me, and then looked at our samovar, the fine silver piece with my initials on the side. She caught me looking at her, smiled, and looked away.

I heard a voice outside, and saw one of the men looking through the window at me. I thought nothing of it, but then heard raised voices. They grew louder.

The woman cast anxious glances at us, then went outside, where her voice joined the others.

'He is burning papers!'

'He is a spy.'

'They are both spies. He is English.'

'But the English are on our side.'

'Whose side? We have no sides.'

'Tell that to the soldiers when they come.'

'And anyway, *she* is Russian.'

I looked at Evgenia, who came over to me.

'What shall we do?'

Then I heard something that made me want to be sick.

'Let's hang them now, to be sure.'

I stood up quickly, and accidentally knocked the samovar over. The old woman must have heard the noise, because she came rushing back inside.

'I'm sorry,' I said. 'We're sorry.'

We set about helping her clear up the mess, when I realised what to do. We had walked into a fairy tale. In fairy tales, there are always tests that must be passed. Challenges to survive. This was one such challenge, and we had to pass it. As in a fairy tale, it was time to cross the old woman's palm with silver.

I winked at Evgenia and then glanced at our precious little samovar. She understood.

'Kind lady,' she said, 'we have troubled you and we should be on our way. Won't you let us leave you the samovar as a gift for your kindness? It is small, but it's very good.'

The old woman was not stupid, she could see what it was worth, never mind its charm. She took it from us eagerly.

We got our things together and were about to leave when the men burst in. But we saw that we had passed the test, because the woman shouted at them and

273

scolded them for their wicked thoughts and inside a minute had sent them scuttling to get our horse ready again.

We went on towards Marienhausen, with only the silence of the forest and the tramp of the horse's hooves for company. Evgenia and I hardly spoke. I put my hand on her knee as I walked beside the cart, but she didn't look down. Her eyes stared into the distance, down the track, and I knew what she was thinking. She was wondering what lay ahead of us; in the forest, and beyond, in the future.

'Are you cold?' I asked as the day wore on.

'No,' she said, smiling, but I could see she was freezing.

'Walk for a bit,' I suggested. 'It'll warm you up.'

A few more miles along the road and we heard the beat of a galloping horse, and then a horseman came into view. We had no idea whose side he was on, but there was a rifle slung across his back.

'Keep walking,' I said to Evgenia and the boy.

The horseman approached, and then to our horror we heard horses behind us. Another twenty or so riders surrounded us before we knew what was happening. Still, I had no idea whose side they were on; they were a motley collection of civil war irregulars, with no uniforms. That gave me an idea. If I didn't know who they were, it stood to reason they didn't know who I was, and I was still wearing my Tsarist officer's greatcoat, after all.

I turned to the nearest man, and fairly barked at him, sounding as angry as I could.

'Have you got an officer with you?'

There was a shaking of heads and I saw my bluff might actually work.

'Are you going to Marienhausen?' I roared, again, trying to seem as disgusted as I could with them.

'Exactly so,' one of them said, adding quickly, 'Your Excellency.'

The coat was doing its job.

'And is there an officer in Marienhausen?'

'No, sir, not at present.'

Excellent news.

'So, on with you, and tell them I am coming! Get rooms ready for my wife and I, and for the boy. We leave in the morning.'

23

'Arthur,' Evgenia whispered to me. 'What have you done?'

She had a point, but I didn't like to admit it. The bluff had worked so far.

At Marienhausen we had been welcomed as an officer should be. I had been invited to inspect the gang of irregulars holding the garrison, an unlikely bunch with half a uniform and about four rifles between them; the other men holding pitchforks and hoes for dear life.

With trepidation I learned that the regular White soldiers, and their officer had left only that morning, leaving this lot behind in the charge of an old non-commissioned officer from Tsarist days.

This had worked in our favour, for he had a strong sense of the deference due a superior, and so we had eaten well and were now sleeping, or trying to sleep, in the old fellow's bed which he had given up for us.

'We ride out at six,' I said, before turning in. 'Have the horse ready and see the boy is fed.'

Now Evgenia and I lay awake, staring at the painted wooden ceiling, trying to ignore the fact there were things moving in the mattress, expecting to hear a crash of boots on the stairs at any time, and feel a noose around our necks a moment later.

'It's all right,' I said, as much to convince myself, as her. 'This is a fairy tale. We're in a fairy tale, and we both know how to live in fairy tales. If we do the right things, say the right things, it will save us.'

'Oh, Arthur, will you ever live in the real world?'

'I will,' I said, quietly, 'we will. Once we find a place to call home. In the meantime all we have to do is keep living the fairy tale. We are a White nobleman and his wife fleeing to the safety of Reval, and if we keep calm and don't seem too eager to get away, it'll be all right.'

It seemed I was right. In the morning we went downstairs to find breakfast and our horse waiting for us. Our boy was very cheerful and said he couldn't remember when he'd had so much to eat.

One of the soldiers came over to me.

'I was thinking,' he said, 'how are things on the other side? With the Reds?'

I shrugged. I had to pretend to know nothing of them.

'Hungry and cold,' I said, 'like us, I suppose.'

The soldier nodded.

'I feel sorry for them. They are just like us. Just

people. We are given food and guns by the English. I don't understand why we aren't at peace with them. Why can't the English make us all make peace?'

The temptation to tell him that one Englishman very close to him was trying to help them make peace was very great, but I resisted. In a fairy tale a foolish tongue can cost its owner much pain.

Our luggage was piled in again and we set off once more, though not without huge relief that the second test was over. The irregular soldiers I had been able to fool; I knew it would not be so easy to talk our way past the real thing, should we meet them.

It wasn't long before we did, but I shouldn't have been surprised; I should have known there had to be the third and final test, or the fairy tale wouldn't have been complete.

It was a fiercely bright morning, but the sun had no strength in it, no warmth. At least we had managed to take an extra blanket or two from the garrison, and Evgenia was firmly wrapped up on top of our bags.

I was walking beside the boy, chatting, trying to stamp some warmth into my feet as I went, when we saw a long column of cavalry riding towards us.

White Army men, with a group of officers riding at the head of the column.

'Arthur!' Evgenia called from the cart. 'What now? What do we do?'

At last, our luck had run out.

As they came within a few yards of us, I opened my mouth to speak, but could think of nothing to say, or do. I would fail the test.

A rider at the front broke away from the others and galloped towards us. With my heart in my mouth I stepped forward to meet him, and raised an arm.

He lifted his arm, I thought to wield his sword, but a second later he pulled up in front of me, waving.

'Ha! I thought it was you,' he said.

I looked at the young officer, who dismounted and came to shake my hand.

'Don't you recognise me?'

There was something familiar about him, it was true. Then, laughing, he hid his moustache with two fingers.

'Better?'

'Yes,' I said. 'Yes, I remember. We met in Galicia, during the war? Yes? Where was it?'

'Tarnopol.'

'Tarnopol! That's it. You're the chess player.'

At last it came back to me. I'd been down at the Galician front, early in the war, reporting for the *News*. I'd met him then and discovered he played chess. We'd had a game in the middle of the field kitchens and tents, the chaos of the camp all around us. That day I'd been lucky, and just as he seemed about to beat me, I'd inflicted a smothered mate on him, a sore defeat.

He'd challenged me to another game, but we'd

been disturbed even as we set up the pieces, and never played it.

'Now,' he said, laughing, 'you can tell me what on earth you're doing here, and we can have that other game of chess.'

There it was, the third test, passed.

But not without one last lesson on how to live in a fairy tale, this time from Evgenia.

Time had not improved the officer's chess skills. Maybe he'd never had the chance to play a single game since that day in Tarnopol, maybe he'd suffered in the war. Whatever the reason, I was beating him easily, and he was getting agitated. When I took his second rook his agitation became anger and he swore at himself.

I looked up to see Evgenia, who'd been watching us play, standing behind him. She fixed my gaze, and then mouthed one word at me.

'Lose,' she said, and I understood. There was a war we were fighting, but this chess match was not it. We needed his help.

But how to do it? Cautiously. It wouldn't do at all to make it too obvious. I let a pawn go and then my queen's knight. I pretended to get flustered and made a couple of reckless moves. Then I showed him my queen and he finished me off in three moves.

He was delighted.

'Ha!' he cried. 'I thought you had me, but now we

are even. One game all. Shall we play a decider?'

'No,' I said, smiling. 'I think we should wait another three years before we play again. And we must get going. We have to get to Reval.'

He stood and saluted me, and then lifted and kissed Evgenia's hand.

'Of course. You will have everything it is in my power to give. We have an officer's railway car on the siding. It is yours when the next train leaves for Reval. I will arrange for the car to join the train. I'm afraid it has cockroaches in it, but it is yours to use.'

24

It was over.

We, Evgenia and I, and the cockroaches, rolled through the Estonian countryside in style, such style as we'd not seen since Lockhart's final party in Moscow, so long ago.

We got to Reval with ease and promptly collapsed, from exhaustion, illness or worry, I don't know which, but one day, I woke up in our beautiful room at the Golden Lion Hotel, and knew that we'd won. We'd won our own little war, to be together, and nothing would ever stop us from being together again.

1942 — Coniston

The years slipped away.

I sit by the fire, and gaze at the empty chair across from me, and listen to the call of the geese down at the water. The shotgun roars, again. It reminds me that the world is at war once more, but I am too old for all that now, too old.

We never were apart again, we never were. Not in all those years.

And later, I wrote, and I wrote furiously, not about men and war, but about children and adventure, and it did my heart good to do it, and maybe, just maybe, it healed the scar left by what happened with Tabitha. I created some children who I would never lose, who would never walk away from me, or be taken. And who I could never walk away from either, for good or bad.

There's a noise from the kitchen and the door opens. Genia comes in with a tray and sits down in the empty chair.

I thought we'd have some tea, she says, in her English still with that dreamy Russian accent. Even now her voice can take me back all those years, to Petrograd, a city that changed its name once more, in honour of the little man with a small and excellent beard, who changed Russia for ever. For better, or for worse. These days they call it Leningrad. This new war has brought soldiers to its door again, and it suffers a terrible siege that I cannot imagine, but I am done with such things. I left politics behind long ago, and I was glad of it.

I often wonder to myself how little we understand our lives, even when we've had the time to pick over the fallen leaves. And if we know so little about our own lives, what does anyone else ever know? All they see is a scant biography, read in a hurry and half-forgotten, as memorable as a footprint in a puddle.

So I forgot politics and soon, politics forgot me.

I sailed instead. We had a boat built. A small one, but then another, much larger. And then a yacht. We sailed the Baltic from east to west and back. One day, we pulled in at an island off the coast of Estonia, a tiny place, that couldn't have changed in a hundred years or more. We had repairs to make to the boat and we found a boat builder. While he worked, I asked him if he'd suffered much during the war.

War? he said. Was there a war?

It made me smile to hear that.

We're nearly out of tea, Evgenia says. Then, Look what I found in the back of the cupboard.

She pulls out something we've both not seen in years. A small case, a strange one, dark green leather, with crimson straps. I remember when I first saw it, pushed across the desk to me, and then we laugh as we remember the next time I saw it, the day we unpacked in Reval, and it fell out of Evgenia's luggage.

What's that? I'd asked, though I'd already guessed what she'd done. Who she'd done a deal with.

You can never go back, I said, and marvelled as I counted thirty-two diamonds and over a hundred pearls.

But now I don't need to go back, she said, and laughed. Because we are together.

We found a way.

We found a way.

Fallen Leaves

Nicholas, Alexandra, Olga, Tatiana, Maria, Anastasia and Alexei Romanov were shot by firing squad in the basement of the 'Ipatiev House' in Ekaterinburg where they were being held, on the night of 16 July 1918. Alexei was still just thirteen, the age at which, according to Rasputin's prediction, the boy's haemophilia would be taken from him forever.

Vladimir Illyich Ulyanov, known as Lenin, remained leader of the Soviet state until his death in 1924.

Lev Davidovich, known as Trotsky, was originally a key player in the Revolution, but later fell foul of Stalin's regime and was exiled. He was brutally murdered by a Spanish communist agent in Mexico in 1940.

Karl Radek, like Trotsky, was also persecuted by Stalin. He was exiled to Tobolsk and it is believed he died in an Arctic labour camp in 1939.

Vatslav Vorovsky was murdered in Switzerland in 1923.

Ants Piip, Estonian Minister, later Head of State, died in a prison camp in 1941.

Robert Bruce Lockhart returned to England and wrote several books of memoirs on the wave of his notoriety.

Arthur Ransome, along with Evgenia Petrovna Shelepina, lived in Estonia and travelled extensively in the Baltic and later in China. They were eventually married on 8 May 1924 at the British Consulate in Reval, Estonia, now Tallinn.

Swallows and Amazons, the first of Ransome's famous adventure stories, was published in 1930.

Author's Note

When I was young my favourite author was Arthur Ransome, though the book I loved the most was not one of the Swallows and Amazons series, but his collection of fairy tales called *Old Peter's Russian Tales*. That book, plus an extraordinary true story, have inspired this book.

This is a work of fiction, but it is very closely based on the real events surrounding Arthur Ransome's time in revolutionary Russia. Nevertheless, in order to tell the story well I found it sensible to modify one or two things; for instance, there is no evidence that Arthur was present the night that Lockhart witnessed Rasputin's infamous performance in the Yar. In more general terms I've used an author's prerogative to make inferences where the facts dry up, and in my defence I'll simply say that this is not a biography, and shouldn't read like one. The vast majority of incidents in this book, however, happened just as I have told them, showing as so often that fact is stranger than fiction. When I came across Ransome's story I'm afraid I found it too

288

good not to tell. After the National Archives released the Secret Service files on Ransome, the new information they revealed only added more mystery to this amazing episode of his life. There's more about the files, as well as some of the memos and telegrams contained in them, in the appendix. I'm indebted to the National Archives for their permission to reproduce them here. I would also like to thank Jane Nissen for the permission to borrow from Ransome's beautiful introduction to *Old Peter's Russian Tales*.

A Timeline

Dates are given according to the Julian Calendar, until 1 February 1918, when Russia adopted the modern Gregorian system. The Julian Calendar ran 13 days behind the Gregorian.

1905

9   January. Bloody Sunday. The Tsar's soldiers fire on the crowd demonstrating in front of the Winter Palace in St Petersburg. The Tsar establishes control once more but in a concessionary move later in the year he is forced to inaugurate Russia's first parliament.

1913

1   June. Arthur Ransome arrives in St Petersburg for the first time.

1914

19 July. Germany declares war on Russia.

1916

16 December. Rasputin is murdered by a group of conspirators led by Prince Felix Yusupov. The extraordinary circumstances of his death become notorious. His death ends his influence over the Tsarina, but is irrelevant to Russia's participation in a disastrous war.

1917

25 February. A general strike in Petrograd and violent clashes between soldiers and workers signal the start of the February Revolution.

7 March. The temporary Government issues a decree for the arrest of Tsar Nicholas II.

3 April. Lenin returns from exile to Petrograd. He arrives at the Finland station to a rapturous welcome and makes a famous speech standing on the bonnet of an armoured car.

25–26 October. Bolshevik guards enter the Winter Palace and assume control of the city and the government.

16 December. Arthur interviews Trotsky and in so doing also meets Evgenia for the first time.

1918

18 January. Robert Bruce Lockhart arrives in Petrograd.

26 February. The Bolsheviks begin to move their government to Moscow, fearing a German invasion

of Petrograd.

Night of 16 July. Execution of the Tsar, his family, and retinue at Ekaterinburg.

5   August. Arthur arrives in Stockholm, having decided that Russia is getting too dangerous, where he is joined on the 28th by Evgenia.

30   August. Lenin narrowly survives an attempt on his life in Moscow. The Red Terror begins and Lockhart is arrested for his part in the alleged 'Lockhart Plot'.

1   October. With Arthur's help, Lockhart is released, and the following day is expelled from Russia for good, leaving behind his mistress, Moura Budberg.

1919

30   January. Having been expelled by the Swedish government from Stockholm under pressure from America and White sympathisers, Arthur and Evgenia return to Russia. At some point during his stay in Stockholm Arthur has been officially designated 'S76' by the SIS. Arthur refers to it as a 'silly proposal' made by Wyatt, a British agent in Stockholm.

4   February. Arthur and Evgenia meet Trotsky and Lenin in Moscow. Trotsky is suspicious of Arthur, treating him as a spy, but Lenin welcomes him warmly.

14   March. Arthur leaves Evgenia behind in Russia, heading for England, where he is arrested on the 25th at King's Cross Railway Station in London. He

is taken to Scotland Yard and questioned by Sir Basil Thomson, head of Special Branch, but later released.

May–September. The White Armies have the upper hand against the Reds and push towards Moscow.

August. Arthur secures a job as correspondent of the *Manchester Guardian*, enabling him to return to Russia, and Evgenia.

Early October. Arthur arrives in Reval, Estonia, and with the help of Assistant Foreign Minister Ants Piip, begins his journey across no man's land into Russia on the 15th.

22 October. Arthur arrives under escort in Moscow and is reunited with Evgenia.

28 October. Arthur and Evegnia leave Moscow, and begin an amazing journey back across no man's land by train, horse and cart, and on foot.

5 November. Arthur and Evgenia arrive safely in Reval, where they check in at the Golden Lion Hotel.

Eighty years after the story ends, a document surfaced in Washington's Library of Congress which claimed that Evgenia had carried a small horde of valuables with her on their epic journey; 32 diamonds and 3 ropes of pearls, their intended use apparently being to further the activities of Bolsheviks outside Russia.

Ransome the Spy?

Secret Service files released by the National Archives on March 1 2005 finally proved that to some extent at least, Arthur Ransome had engaged in secret activities for the SIS.

The files themselves are a confusing tangle of the memos flying around the various, still nascent, departments of the Secret Service, and the F.O. They do prove that AR had a codename (S76) and that he did do some work for the SIS, but also that he was suspected of being a Bolshevik agent by many. I think the truth lies in the middle: he worked for the British, and possibly also helped the Bolsheviks. For example, we know that Arthur was sent by Trotsky on a shopping expedition around Petrograd, but this was no idle shopping trip. Trotsky, albeit a legendary revolutionary, was at the start of the Revolution largely ignorant of the technicalities of warfare. He asked Arthur, who was making a trip from Moscow to check on his old flat in Petrograd, to visit some bookshops and purchase a long list of books on the theory of war. This Arthur did, and unwittingly or not was therefore responsible for helping Trotsky to create the Red Army.

It's important to consider the nature of what we are talking about: spying across Europe at the time was in its infancy. In Britain, the various departments had just been established: the Secret Service Bureau had been split into home and foreign departments in 1910. MI5 was, as now, the home section, under the control of Captain Vernon Kell. MI6 however was known as MI1c during the war but by the end of the war was known as the SIS. Its first head was Captain Mansfield Cumming, or 'C' (the head of MI6 is still called 'C' from this time). There was rivalry between these departments and also with Special Branch, who all saw Bolshevik spies as their responsibility. Special Branch was run by Sir Basil Thomson who makes a brief appearance in Part 3 of the novel when he interrogates AR on his return from Russia in March 1919.

Spies at the time were few and far between and many of them were not professional 'agents' but men in certain places who were asked to provide whatever information they could. This might be an English journalist or businessman, whose work took them to foreign parts, where they could observe and comment on, for example, the German fleet size. It really was like a gentleman's club, full of eccentric behaviour and few rules of engagement – one German spy refused to pass on information except via 'pretty girls', and the technology of information transfer was often primitive – knitting patterns in a newspaper were used as a code in one instance.

In Lockhart's case, Embassy staff were the perfect weapon of choice as they were largely immune from investigation by the 'enemy', being diplomats. Ransome fitted the bill of someone who just happened to have close contact with the Bolsheviks, more than any other Englishman, and so what the SIS might term spying was in reality just a question of passing on information that no one else had. I suspect it went little further than this – a question of charming people, saying the right things, asking the right questions, and passing this information back to the UK. What is more interesting is whether Ransome or Evgenia really left Russia with 3 million roubles of Bolshevik money.

Appendix

Memo 294084/M. I. 5. E.

8th July 1918

My dear [blank passage]

With reference to F. O. telegram No. 301 of 21/6/18 from Moscow concerning the useful lady whom they wish to send to Stockholm and who will go as Ransome's official wife. We have informed F. O. that there is no military objection.

However for your information I am informed very reliably that Ransome has applauded the Bolsheviks to such an extent in his newspaper writing that one is almost forced to the conclusion that he is a Bolshevik himself.

It would probably be worth while to keep an eye on the lady and see what her activities really are.

Yours sincerely,

S.

M. I. 5. E

CX. 050167

P/F. 84.   Stockholm, 12-9-18

I do not know how much is known in London of Arthur Ransome's activities here, or whether his dispatches are being allowed to go through and be published in the Daily News, but it certainly ought to be understood how completely he is in the hands of the Bolsheviks.

He seems to have persuaded the Legation that he has changed his views to some extent but this is certainly not the case. He claims, as has already been reported to you, to be the official historian of the Bolshevik movement. I suppose this is true, at all events it is true that he is living here with a lady who was previously Trotsky's private secretary, that he spends the greater part of his time in the Bolshevik Legation, where he is provided with a room and a typewriter, and that he is very nervous as to the effect which his present activities may have upon his prospects in England.

I also know that he had informed two Russians that I, personally, am an agent of the British Government, and said that he had this information from authoritative sources, both British and Bolshevik.

He seems therefore to be working pretty definitely against us.

ENDS

SECRET

M. I. 5

29th October 1918

RANSOME, Arthur

Ref. B/02277, dated 25-9-18

I sent you then CX. 050167, (P/F. 84 Stockholm, dated 12-9-18).

Our political section has from the same agent a later report written to correct the P/F. 84. In this it is stated that Ransome seems to have been quite badly handled, that he is quite loyal and willing to help by giving information, and that the appearance of working against us is due to his friendship with the Bolshevik leaders, not by any means to any sympathy with the regime, which the Terror has made him detest.

We expect to get a lot of most valuable stuff from him and it is hoped that you will see your way, so to speak, to leave him alone for a bit and give him a chance. Mr Lockhart has an extremely good opinion, and has strongly recommended Stockholm to make use of him.

Major, M. I. 1. c

P. P. 459/M. I. 5. E. 1.

The following is a list of 13 Russian Bolsheviks with their descriptions and photographs, who are operating in Stockholm. They are probably going to be compelled to leave Sweden by the Swedish Government.

None of them are to have visas for, or to land in, the United Kingdom.

Vorovsky, Vatslav, Russian, Stockholm. Long black hair, brushed back; straight nose; full beard and moustache; sharp black eyes, about 42-45 years.

Litvinov, Maxim, Russian, Stockholm. Smooth shaven, dark hair, dishevelled, brushed back, wears pince-nez, thick set.

Sepp, Otto, Russian, Stockholm. Closely-cropped hair; small moustache; energetic-looking face with fanatic look in the eyes.

Ransome, Arthur, British, Stockholm. Hair parted on left side; narrow, shrewd eyes; wears pince-nez.

London

17th March 1919

Memo from S8 regarding Arthur Ransome (S76)

I do not think that, pending investigation, much credence should be attached to the various reports which have been made regarding any definite activities which S76 is alleged to have engaged in on behalf of the Bolsheviks.

I have not had the opportunity of questioning him personally regarding the earlier statement that he carried a large quantity of Roubles out of Russia for the Bolsheviks, but from everything I know of the nature of his relations with the Bolsehviks, I think it impossible in the extreme that he ever did anything of the kind consciously.

I would suggest that he be allowed to enter England without any difficulties or any suggestions that he is regarded as a suspicious person.

S8

Copies to M. I. 5

D. C. I.

SECRET

PF. R. 301/M. I. 5. E. 1.

18th December 1918

<u>RANSOME, Arthur</u>

Reference PF.R.301 of 8/11/18

The above will shortly be arriving from Stockholm. We have received the following regarding him:

[blank passage]

There is of course no objection to an ordinary search when he arrives. We cannot guarantee him, but, it is suggested that there is no fear of him bringing in secret ink, so that the more trying methods might be omitted.

For information.

Captain

Copies to:- Aberdeen. Newcastle.

Arthur RANSOME

Arthur Ransome arrived in England 3 days ago. He was expelled from Sweden by the Government on account of his Bolshevist activities, and with the Bolshevist Legation to Sweden (Vorovsky and Litvinoff (formerly of London), which was expelled at the same time, returned to Moscow with his mistress in January 1919.

M. I. thought his opinions were all camouflage. Our evidence goes all the way to prove that it was not so.

R was in Moscow until 20th January this year, with his mistress, with whom he has been living since December 1917, a Russian Jewess, who, when R was in Moscow at the earlier date had been put on him to complete the 'catch' of this useful foreign correspondent, by Trotzky, whose secretary she was!

R reached the country and landed unhindered. The following questions seem pertinent:

Was Arthur Ransome searched when he arrived in this country?

What messages and letters did he bring from Bolshevik HQ Moscow to this country? And to whom were they delivered?

Telegram

W. O. No. 02501

eighteenth on special request British
Consul Ransome received Visa Swedish Legation
extraquick time STOP Ransome's character
should be known London undoubtedly capable
dangerous agent

304